# Shrugg
# 1 Mile

### G. A. Schindler

Copyright © 2014 G. A. Schindler

first edition

edited by Amanda Brown

cover design by G. A. Schindler

All rights reserved.

ISBN-10:1502999420
ISBN-13:978-1502999429

## CONTENTS

Acknowledgments

1 The Mugging 5

2 The Hugging 13

3 Allways Saturdaze 23

4 Begin The Trip 32

5 Shrugg, 1 Mile 39

6 Treed In Shrugg 46

7 Meet Magoo 52

8 Shrugg 61

9 More Hugging 80

10 Band Aids R Green 89

Writer's Blog....................97

I'd like to thank Chris Kwapich, who helped me get the ball pen rolling and my wife, Susanna, who helped me keep it rolling.

# ~ 1 ~

## THE MUGGING

Mark locked the heavy kitchen door and dragged his feet across the empty parking lot. His Chevy looked dejected sitting alone in the back row by the dumpster where employees parked. He totally agreed that customers should get the closer parking spaces, except when he was dead tired after a double shift and trudging across the lot seemed a major chore. Usually the manager and an assistant manager closed up the restaurant and walked to their cars parked side by side. Tonight he was alone. Tom had used a sick day because Julie was in labor. Mark hoped it was going well. They had three daughters. He hoped they caught a break and got the son they wanted.

A few shuffling steps from his car, Mark heard a small noise by the dumpster. From the corner of his eye, he thought he saw a movement. The moon was thinly clouded over. There was too little light to make anything out. Then a shadow separated from the dumpster--a man walking toward him--not the cute raccoon or somewhat alarming black bear he'd expected. The man was tall with massive shoulders. His wide-brimmed hat cast a shadow that rendered him faceless. The words "headless horseman" skittered across the back of Mark's mind.

Rushing to use his keys, Mark fumbled them. The sound rang loudly.

"Say, ya got a bit a cash ya could spare a hungry stranger, mister?" the faceless hat, now nearly at arm's length, asked down at him in a strangely, soft voice.

*A guy his size doesn't need a booming bass voice to get what he wants*, Mark thought. This huge fellow sounded like Peter Lorre acting the roll of a pirate.

"I, I, I dropped my keys."

"I heared that. I asked have you got any spare cash ta help a poor soul?"

"N-n-n-o. I'm broke. Tomorrow's payday."

"Hmmmm. Ya *know* I could kill ya, don't ya?"

With that, Mark wetted himself. They both smelled it.

"I'm a bettin' man, an' I got a dollar says yer lyin'. I'm gonna put this buck right here in yer pocket. Y'll have ta excuse it's a bit damp. Hell, I'll even throw ya in this little souvenir too."

Mark thought he saw hair in the dark hand that stuffed something into his shirt pocket.

"There, that's yours ta keep no matter what. Now hand me the wallet. I'm gonna trade ya fer whatever cash is in yer wallet. If you ain't lied, I'm gonna apologize an' yer gonna come outta this a whole buck ahead. Won't ya be the lucky one?"

Mark hesitated.

"Ya know this knife could slice right through yer throat or slip real easy into yer belly. I'd give ya the choice. Ya might survive the gut shot if I don't twist too much or happen ta hit nothin' vital, but it'll hurt more. The neck is quick an' merciful."

"Ok-k-kay, okay." Mark blubbered.

He fumbled for his wallet.

"Well, I find four bills in here, but I can't see the size. D' ya spose you could fill me in on the size? How much did yer lyin' cost ya mister?"

"I'm p-p-pretty sure it's a twenty, aaaand two tens an' a one."

"Well, that was an expensive lie, wasn't it?"

Mark didn't say anything.

"Wasn't it?" he repeated just as softly.

"Yeah."

"A dollar's worth o' charity an' I would 've been glad ta see yer heart was in the right place. A fiver woulda made ya my hero. Now step back."

He stepped back against his car and the man reached down and picked up his dropped keys."

"Now turn round."

He heard his wallet drop. His knees went weak and nearly buckled as he turned. Was he breathing his last? Tears rolled down his cheeks.

His tossed keys landed somewhere far out on the parking lot, seemingly near the restaurant building.

"That'll take ya while. I coulda' threw 'em in the bushes an' you'd be all night lookin'." With that he turned and walked toward the dumpster.

Mark heard his footsteps and turned as clouds cleared from the three-quarter moon. He viewed the man's receding back for three seconds, his eyes glued in disbelief to the gross discrepancy between those stilt-like legs, elongated arms swinging down to the knees and that mashed down body, short as it was wide with even wider shoulders. It all seemed put together like a caricature of an orangutan. He flashed on an Edgar Allen Poe story where a trained orangutan was the murderer.

The figure disappeared behind the dumpster and Mark hurried around to his car's right, rear wheel-well to retrieve the magnetic box with its spare key. In a New York minute, he was behind the steering wheel with doors locked. Finally feeling a little safer, he leaned back and sucked in a deep breath. His hands began shaking, and the urine smell was strong.

His assailant had apparently tossed his keys across the lot to buy time, yet in less than a minute Mark was ready to roll. But in which direction? For a few crazy seconds he considered driving toward the dumpster. If the guy needed time, he hadn't gotten it. Now Mark had the advantage of surprise if he moved quickly.

But then again surprise was all he had. He could drive around the dumpster. The car was a weapon but it was hard to justify running down somebody who hadn't touched you or even shown you any type of weapon. Was forty bucks worth killing somebody over even if they did scare the piss out of you quite literally? What the hell *was* that big thing? Had some*body*, or some*thing* scared him? Was he even safe from it inside his car?

Mark turned and drove slowly through the parking lot near the restaurant until he spied the keys in his headlights. He slowed, opened his door, leaned down and scooped them up without touching a foot to the pavement. Then he peeled out, spewing gravel.

On his way home he decided not to call the police. It was an easy decision. He'd seen no face he could describe and no weapon. He had no real evidence. Who'd believe his description of a soft-spoken SpongeBob SquarePants on stilts with football shoulder pads and arms four feet long? He could close his eyes and see it, yet there was no way even *he* could believe it. They'd laugh and think he was on drugs or something. He was awfully tired after a double shift and it all began to take on a dreamlike quality. Reaching up to his shirt pocket he felt the crumpled dollar, still damp and still very real.

During the robbery, Mark had managed to maintain some semblance of calm. Now flashes of it kept running and rerunning uncontrolled through his mind. He was coming unglued. While he gripped the wheel, his hands quit shaking. When he pried them off the wheel they started again. Unlocking his front door wasn't easy. His hands didn't stop shaking until he'd been in bed under the covers for several minutes balled up in a fetal position. It was a warm night, damned near summer, yet he fell asleep shivering under a quilt.

He awoke near seven, every muscle in his body aching as he swayed, nearly falling, into the bathroom. It was all a dream that had to go away. He was making too much of it. So he'd been mugged. People got mugged all the time. There were lots of weirdly shaped people in the world. This guy, or thing, whoever or whatever it was, hadn't so much as touched him. He'd never seen any knife. The guy probably didn't even have a knife. Of course he had the urine-soaked pants and the damp dollar bill to prove it was no dream, but he had to man up and get over it.

In the middle of brushing his teeth the word "souvenir" jumped into Mark's mind. The guy had said he was putting a souvenir in his pocket with the dollar. It wasn't there. It must have fallen out when he leaned over to pick up the keys. He vaguely remembered hearing something fall. Damn. He checked the shirt pocket in case this souvenir was small enough for him to have missed. No. Yet how badly did he really want some friggin keepsake from last night. Likely not much, but he damn well wanted to know what the hell it was before he tossed it. So he got dressed hurriedly.

His wallet was still there too--where the stranger dropped it. Mark had remembered it on his way home and figured some coworker would find it this morning and leave it on his desk. It wasn't enough to get him back anywhere near that parking lot last night in the dark. This morning, in the light of day, the lost wallet was a good excuse to poke around the back lot looking for that souvenir, whatever the hell it might be.

The breakfast customers were all parked out front. He left his car beside the building. The back lot was empty except for four employee cars and the cook's motorcycle in a row by the dumpster. Mark scanned the empty fields all around, wondering where the strange figure had come from. The grass wasn't quite knee high. Where would he plan to hide after his heist? He most likely ran a bit, then laid flat, hidden by the darkness. Or he may have run a hundred yards to the trees, then went on to follow the railroad tracks that came across through the woods. He hadn't given Mark the impression he could move very fast. He seemed kind of old-slow. Right now he could be staring at Mark from that bright morning green, innocent looking tree line. Mark hoped he was far away though. Police dogs might be able to track him down but it was hardly worth all the trouble for forty lousy bucks.

Mark scoured the parking lot with a nervous eye on the distant woods, and found only a small pen. It seemed to be the object of his quest. About three inches long, it was just a cheap plastic one with no way to retract or protect the long ink cartridge tip. It was a glowing opalescent white, with "Shrugg Inn" printed on it in a script font. Mark studied it. It wasn't fancy but seemed brand new--totally unblemished by last night's rough treatment. Where the hell was the Shrugg Inn? He put it in his pocket, then scanned the tree line once more.

Mark went in through the kitchen door. He'd long since decided not to tell anyone at the restaurant about last night's bone-chilling scare. They'd think he was off his rocker or on drugs. His movement up the management ladder would come to a screeching halt.

The first thing he heard was Jimmy, the cook, say, "Hey dude, your wallet's on your desk. I found it in the parking lot."

"Yeah, thanks. I was hoping it was here somewhere."

"You're lucky it didn't rain last night."

"Yeah, thanks again. I've gotta be more careful."

Mark went to his desk, picked up his wallet, then ducked back out the kitchen door. He was glad not to see anyone. It was hard to act relaxed and normal. He knew he must look like death warmed over. If anyone asked about his appearance, he might be unable to hold back-- break down and spill it all out.

Back in the car Mark called Beth. He wanted to see her. She was the one he could talk to. She answered after the third ring, sounding like she might have been asleep.

"Hi, Mark."

"Hi. Sorry to call early. Hope I didn't wake you."

"No. I've been awake a while. I'm just curled up in bed doing some reading. One class today. It's at eleven. What's up?"

"Well, I haven't eaten anything yet and something kinda crazy happened last night. I need to talk about it. Could we go out to breakfast?"

"I don't want to get dressed and go out, but I've got bagels and lots of eggs. Come by and let's eat here."

"Are you sure you don't mind?"

"No. I'd love it, as long as you give me time to brush my teeth. What happened last night? Are you okay?"

"Yeah. I'm not hurt or anything. Don't wanna talk about it on the phone. I just left the Daze, so I'll be by in about twenty minutes if that isn't too quick."

"That'll do. How do you like your eggs?"

"Scrambled with a little onion if you've got any."

"Yeah. I've got cheese too. If you want mushrooms, you can pick some up on the way."

Mark liked mushrooms but couldn't make any stops. "Onions and cheese sound great. See ya shortly."

"Okay. You sound a littllllle....different. Drive careful."

"Sure. I'm okay."   {~ 1 ~}

## ~ 2 ~

## THE HUGGING

Mark and Beth had met two months before at the restaurant. Beth had gone there for her first meal in town after a long day's work making her new apartment livable. They'd been seeing each other a lot and were at that delicate point where each was pretty certain of their own feelings, yet a bit uncertain of the other's. For both there was a hesitancy borne of past disappointment

Over breakfast he poured out the story. Everything but him wetting his pants.

"I feel so tired. Every muscle I have aches. When I got home last night I just undressed and fell into bed. I only slept because I was dead tired after a double shift. I was wound up like a spring. This morning I felt like I stayed wound up all night. It has to be the worst sleep I've ever had. Then I remembered that souvenir and my wallet, so I threw on some clean clothes and headed back there. Jeez I really need a shower. I'd better get back home. Maybe we can meet for lunch to talk about…"

"No." Beth interrupted, "you need to take a nice hot relaxing shower here. Then we'll talk."

He started to say no, but it sounded so right and inviting that he acquiesced.

His appearance had grown pale, and Beth had heard such change in his voice as he blurted out the story that she feared there was even more to it than the terribly disturbing events he'd described.

Recounting the experience with Beth brought all the intense fear back to Mark, but at the same time he felt he was breathing it out of him, as he remembered a huge man in *The Green Mile* breathing out spirits. Now the hot water magically began washing the ache from his muscles. He heard a tap on the door. Then it opened.

"I think another towel would be good," Beth said.

The shower curtain was opaque, so she wasn't invading his privacy. He was listening for the door to close when he heard the curtain slide over a little and she stepped in behind him. Beth wrapped her arms around Mark, pressed herself to him, leaned forward on her tiptoes and said, "I love you," in his ear.

He turned, put his arms around her and whispered in her ear, "I love you, I love you. I soooo love you."

As his hands slowly slid down her back, he released a sigh as though the weight of the world was lifting from his shoulders.

When they finished he began to cry. Softly, then louder in sobs. The fear and tension from the night before was releasing and washing down the drain. Tears welled up in Beth's eyes. She had to bring him back, resuscitate the man she knew. Replace, if only for a fleeting while, those overwhelming fears he'd felt. They embraced until he calmed and his body no longer shook. She kissed him, whispered, "I love you," in his ear and then enjoyed taking a long, leisurely while fulfilling his fondest dream.

Beth skipped class. They spent much of the day in her bed speaking little, experiencing the luxurious new physicality of each other. Their curious eyes and fingertips enjoyed leisurely exploration and they basked in being lovingly explored.

They stayed in and had grilled cheese sandwiches and chicken noodle soup for lunch. She told him of her two high school, fumbling drive-in nights--the total of her sexual experience.

"A drive-in movie. Is there really one of those left standing?" Mark smiled.

"I told you I came from a small town. As far as I know the Pioneer Drive-In, just outside Coopersville is still showing movies. I don't think it's the last one in the world standing, but close to it."

Mark told of his sexual experience, explaining he was ten months from the pain of his first and only soul mate, whose promise of forever lasted only two years. They were great, short years that left a bitterness.

"I'm sorry if you wanted a virgin." She apologized.

"No, I'm not…"

"I thought about faking it, but honesty has to be better. Actually my eyes are quite virgin. It's dark in those drive-ins and you can't take many clothes off either. The most fun was the second time when I walked to the concession stand during intermission so naughty naked under my dress. Then we went up to the kid's playground. We were the only ones there. I sat on a swing facing the screen, away from all the cars. He stood in front, pushing me higher, staring as my skirt billowed up. It was a hot night but the air felt cool coming up under my dress. The air rushing up and that amazed excited look in his eyes, were so awesome. Anyway, it's all been so long ago that I must have earned my virginity back by now. I've become pickier. Nobody's been even near third base since then. Haven't had any boyfriends I've felt that close to."

Finally they got dressed for dinner. It was a short walk to Joey's Crazy Pizza where, in a corner booth, they finally got back to discussing the five hundred pound gorilla in the corner of room--a gorilla which had mercifully blended chameleon-like into the wallpaper throughout the beautiful warm glow of their day. Mark recounted every astounding detail of the ordeal this time, but more slowly and in a voice that told Beth he was stronger and getting beyond the fear. When he mentioned wetting his pants she heard the slight hesitance of shame in his voice.

"I'm surprised it took you so long." She threw in, "I'd have lost it when I saw him walking toward me."

That morning Beth had thought Mark's description of his assailant was perhaps a product of his fear, the poor lighting, and some deceptive clothing the tall man wore. Now she wasn't so certain and she shivered. As he finished she asked, "Can I see the pen?"

He pulled it from his pocket.

"Kinda *different*, isn't it?" she said, inspecting it. "Wonder how well it writes."

She found some paper in her purse. The pen wrote as smooth as butter with the feel of a really expensive pen. As the long tip glided so smoothly across the paper the pen seemed to glow a bit, tingling her fingertips ever so slightly. It felt as though there might be something related to a jumping bean inside. But there seemed no way to open it to look inside without breaking it.

"Makes you really wonder where the Shrugg Inn is, doesn't it?" Beth said. "We'll have to Google it."

"Yeah." Mark agreed. "Can't say I'd be too anxious to go there though. Might like to learn the location just to know I was staying as far away as possible.

"You know, I'd just figure he was some bum out there riding trains or walking the tracks, if it wasn't for his unbelievable shape and this strange pen. It seems too unique to be any accident. He put the dang thing in my pocket and told me he was putting it there. How much more deliberate can you be? Considering how new it looks after the beating it took last night, I can't imagine what it would take to break it open."

"What about the dollar he put in your pocket? Was there anything unusual about it?"

"I don't know. It's still in the pocket of my dirty shirt. I'll look it over when I get home."

"Well, we can do the Nancy Drew thing a bit and go hunting around for clues Mark, but if we find anything maybe we should let the police know."

"You know, part of me feels like something *should* be done about the whole weird incident, because if he gets away with it, he could really hurt somebody the next time. But I don't want to tell anyone about it yet. The whole thing was too small potatoes and unbelievable for anyone to take seriously. A big part of me says just forget about it, I'd just be tagged a nut case. Let's go over to my place, Google Shrugg Inn and check out that dollar bill."

Mark's fear of setting himself up for ridicule, and the almost certainty of being labeled unstable (code word for unpromotable) by the Allways Saturdaze restaurant chain would have been enough reason for him to keep his story to himself. There was more to his reluctance, though. He didn't really know if he wanted to bring the wrath of the world down on his strange assailant. The bazillionth time the incident replayed itself through his mind's eye, Mark's feelings about the guy and their encounter had begun to wobble.

First off was the voice. It was so Peter Lorre mixed with small hints of Morgan Freeman. The absurd pirate imitation absolutely put it over-the-top hilarious, when you got past the fear of what was said. Then there was the wide, flat-rimmed Clint Eastwood cowboy hat. The whole confrontation had come directly out of a poorly written spaghetti western. That was an oxymoron. A spaghetti western spoof is what it was.

He doubted the old guy really had a knife, and suspected that he'd been nearly as scared as Mark. He might have been wearing some kind of mask. Perhaps a black stocking mask that covered his entire head with only small openings for eyes and mouth.

The whole thing may not have been about taking any money, but rather giving away the pen. The idea that any modicum of charity on Mark's part would have been a deal breaker didn't seem too unlikely either. The pen might have been Mark's gift of appreciation, had things gone differently. But who'd expect a friendly encounter wearing a get up like that in the middle of the night? Especially in such a location. The physique was impossible to fathom. A circus midget on stilts wearing football shoulder pads would almost do. The guy did walk slowly, but not as though he was actually on stilts. Then there were the arms. How could you figure those super long arms?

The old guy had imagination and moxie though, no doubt about it. Then again Mark realized that this take on the encounter was purely conjecture. Instinctively it felt probably right, but could be a hundred and eighty degrees off. Likely he'd never know.

Beth found his story amazing and puzzling. More than anything, she was relieved that it was over and he'd come through it safe and sound. Tonight he seemed a lot more sound. The incident was intriguing but seemed destined to fade into the past as an inexplicable mystery. So all-in-all she was more intrigued by today's exciting turn in their relationship--a relationship she doubted was destined to fade into the past as long as they lived.

Her two teenage sexual forays had been miserable disappointments. Not only had each main event been too brief and unsatisfying, the nice cozy relationships she'd expected to follow hadn't materialized. Instead of the beginning of something warm and exciting, each was a brief forgettable one-nighter which unfortunately she couldn't easily forget. The fact that she never knew why they fizzled didn't help any either. She supposed she'd chosen guys more into conquests than relationships. One alternative--that she had not measured up in some way--had niggled ever since in a remote corner of her mind, an uncomfortable corner to say the least.

Mark didn't show that swarthy Adonis look, great height, chiseled muscle and smiley overconfidence that movies presented as the ideal in spite of miserable drive-in movie experiences with such. He *was* tall, but with short, dark curly hair, and thin to a fault. His narrow face and slightly oversized beak seemed designed with horn rimmed glasses in mind, though he lacked them…so far. His lack of inflated ego Beth particularly appreciated, sensing a truer strength of self-awareness. She saw it coming out in flashes, like flint striking steel, in his writing. With encouragement, he'd become a writer if he stayed at it.

This life-changing day with him left her body just a skosh unsettled though. She couldn't eat much pizza. Her stomach was that of a passenger belted into an airplane tilting, defying gravity, and surging up from the tarmac. She hoped their relationship had been taxiing on the runway just long enough. Taxi too long and you reach the end, crash and burn. Too short and you might just lack the magic momentum. This surge felt fabulous. She'd been humming "Rocket Man" all afternoon. He was her rocket man. What a nice rocket she thought and smiled.

They exited Joey's side by side, Mark's arm over her shoulder and Beth's arm around his waist. He somewhat tall and she a bit short, it was a comfortable fit. The sun was in the final stage of setting, and the streets were deeply shadowed and deserted. Approaching her apartment building he felt a slim, cool hand wander to the middle of his back, then slip easily under his belt and beneath the elastic of his briefs.

An hour later they headed for his place. Beth threw a few books and an overnight bag into her car. They drove separately. They'd need both cars in the morning.

"If you'll boot up the computer, I'll find that dollar bill," Mark said as his front door swung back. "Sorry about the mess. You'll need markkwapich@imagine.scifi and juniordawg to get on."

His apartment was a bit messy, but she'd seen worse. In fact most of the singles' apartments she'd seen--guys' or girls'--were pretty gross. Her own place sometimes got out of hand around exam time.

She was typing Shrugg Inn into Google when Mark came back into the living room. Both the dollar bill and

Shrugg Inn seemed to be dead ends. There was no Shrugg Inn anywhere Beth looked on the computer, and after smoothing all the wrinkles out of it, Mark scrutinized every millimeter of the dollar under a magnifying glass before announcing he could find nothing unusual about it. He'd carefully compared it to a couple other singles from his wallet.

"But why is it still damp?" Beth asked. She held it up, and it hung limp.

"Well, it's been wadded up in my sweaty shirt pocket 'til now, but the shirt seemed to dry out. That guy did say it was damp though when he put it in there."

Beth held it to her nose.

"Does it smell?"

"I think so, just a little."

Mark held it to his nose a long while.

"I don't smell anything."

Beth took it back and smelled it a longer with her eyes closed.

"It's just a really faint kinda sweet smell that I don't think I've ever smelled before. It's so faint I'm not really sure of that. But I'm sure it's there."

He tried smelling it again.

"How come I can't smell it?"

"I've heard us girls have more sensitive noses. Maybe so."

"Since it was damp when I got it, the smell must be some after shave or cologne mixed with that guy's sweat. I bet there's some identifiable DNA on this bill."

"And likely some fingerprints on that pen too, but I'm afraid your strange stranger failed to commit a crime heinous enough to warrant any big police investigation."

"Yeah. I guess it amounts to me buying a forty dollar pen and a sweaty dollar bill. Kind of an expensive pen."

"Works nice though, love."

"Smooth as butter." Mark answered smiling. It was the first time she'd called him that. He liked it,…a lot.

He absently wrote his name a few times with the pen, feeling that slightest tingle in his fingertips, like the purr of a sleeping cat. It was nearly time for bed and he was a happy camper not to sleep alone. He set the alarm early enough to give them time to perhaps try out his shower. Sure enough, the next morning it worked every bit as well as her shower had.  {~ 2 ~}

# ~ 3 ~

## ALLWAYS SATURDAZE

Mark thought about preserving the evidence--pressing the bill between pieces of glass to save the DNA and hiding the pen away to save finger prints--but if they ever caught the guy for something really serious, what could this little punk robbery mean? He did press the bill between glass and put it away anyway, just in case. He also decided to post a note on the employee bulletin board saying a stranger had been seen out back by the tree line, to alert employees not to walk to their car alone after dark. He'd also talk to Tom about having the employee's park at the other end of the back row, away from the dumpster. In fact he'd suggest they put up a barrier to stop anyone from parking near the dumpster. Besides this apparent hobo, there was the occasional black bear, coyote or skunk to consider. You could hardly warn customers about a stranger in the area without possibly scaring them away and losing business, but keeping everyone a short distance from the dumpster seemed a plausible precaution.

When he got to work, Mark parked beside Tom's car by the dumpster. Though it had been a depth of fear he'd never expected to feel in his lifetime, he'd pretty much gotten past it. He did study the tree line before getting out of his car though, then glanced back once as he walked a tad more quickly than usual across the parking lot.

Allways Saturdaze was pretty quiet, as it usually was when he came in between the morning and lunch crowds.

"Hey, Tom had a boy." He heard from Dave the waiter as he passed through the kitchen.

"Great. He must be flying high."

"Sure is. It's like he toked some joints or something."

"Oh! I've never seen him like that before."

"That's 'cause we know he don't smoke that shit an' he's never had no boy child before. You'll see in a sec."

Actually Mark *had* known Tom back in the day when he smoked that shit a few times--something you *didn't* divulge to employees. Dave was right, Tom looked pretty much as he had back then. Mark knew he was just high on fatherhood. It was post-partum euphoria. He'd arrived shortly before Mark and was walking about handing out cellophane-wrapped chocolate cigars with blue ribbons that said "It's a boy!" He was distributing them to employees and customers alike, laughing and grinning as though he'd just won the lottery. Mark was happy for him. His family was complete. He'd confided to Mark that he and Julie were unsure whether they'd try again if this one turned out to be their fourth girl.

Of course it was going to be a party day. He and Tom would get little paper work done. Correct that, Tom would get little paper work done. He'd spend pretty much all day on the floor. It was good for business though. Anything positive and exciting was good to share. It gave folks something to talk and laugh about-- put them all in good spirits, employees and customers.

He and Tom stayed up nights trying to think up new reasons and ways to celebrate at the "Daze". Tom's wife having a baby was a no-brainer. They could stretch it out two or three days once Tom got some good pictures of Julie and the kid to put up on the big screen. Tom would put up news bulletins too. Mark saw he already had the kid's stats up there--seven pounds, six ounces, twenty-two inches, not much hair.

"Hey Mark!" Tom called across the room. .

"Congrats old boy!" Mark shouted. "You did it!"

They hurried together, shook hands and hugged

"Thanks, dude. It doesn't really get any easier the fourth time around. Here have a cigar."

Mark accepted a chocolate cigar and got the whole room going on a rousing "For He's a Jolly Good Fellow."

As they finished he announced: "Of course we're singing this song about his kid. This guy here is such a total bum for putting his wife through all that again. But I guess we'll forgive him. And I suppose she will too. What the hell, I think she did the first three times. A toast to Tom. What a guy. Raise your glasses high. May his next ten kids all be boys so he can have a football team and three cheerleaders," Everybody cheered.

"Thanks a lot, Mark. That's all I'd need, fourteen kids. As much as I like football, it's not gonna happen. If Julie heard you say that, she'd likely shoot you dead on the spot. But don't worry, we keep guns away from her."

"Oh, I heard you don't trust each other with weapons."

"No. We don't even keep a sharp knife in the house."

"I bet that makes carving up the old Thanksgiving turkey quite a wrestle."

After a little more good hearted banter, Mark retired to his cubicle to get going on some paper work. Using his new, very expensive pen, he finished last week's employee time sheets quite quickly. Then he wrote out the employee warning notice about the suspicious stranger and not going out to the parking lot alone after dark. He'd talk with Tom before telling employees to park away from the dumpster. He tacked the notice to the very center of the bulletin board. There were a few more things on his desk that wanted his attention, but he felt really wiped out and unable to concentrate on work. His placid life had exploded into such turmoil in the last two days. He was simultaneously tired to the core, both physically and mentally, and geeked up.

The automatic loop of the incident had quit running itself across his mind and there was nothing new to think about on that front. So of course his thoughts turned to the new development in his life that had him geeked--the awesome change in his relationship with Beth. He couldn't help but compare her to Pat, the only other love of his life. Neither was a raving beauty, but he liked both their looks. Pat had been taller and skinny, giggly and more talkative. Beth had a better figure and was a bit more reserved, except in the bedroom. He loved her long, dark red hair and the way her mouth and light green eyes always seemed to be smiling just a bit. And he liked that she took his writing more seriously. She'd been glad to read several of his short stories and offered some thoughtful suggestions. He was self-conscious about lacking any college training but felt certain his writing had been improving since he joined a local writers' workshop group. Pat's interest had seemed minimal, and she'd never said anything but that his stories were nice. Beth was encouraging and even suggested that with a few changes he could turn the one story into the beginning of a book. He didn't feel ready to tackle a book yet, but when he did, he might take her suggestion.

Mark wondered what they might do about new living arrangements. It was clear that neither of them wanted to sleep alone, but their apartments were inconveniently far apart, and both apartments were too small for them to share comfortably. Was it too soon to go looking for a larger apartment together? He thought not, but she might think so. Near her school would be nice but that area was a bit pricey. He liked it though--liked being around students and the halls of academe. The student energy and exuberance around campus energized him whenever he was there. He was sure it would spur him on to more and better writing. About half the members of his writing group were students at Beth's school and he felt only two were noticeably better writers than him. They were quite a nice, friendly group.

Mark couldn't believe that he and Beth had actually discussed their previous sexual experiences. He didn't think any couples ever did that. It was always a taboo topic as far as he knew. Rule number one--don't mention old flames. Yet she had introduced the topic, they had confided with such ease and it had been so pleasant. It made him feel that theirs would be an open and unusually comfortable relationship, endearing and enduring. They would be able to talk about anything. He'd had no idea of Pat's experience before they met, and he never divulged to her that she was his first. He'd been a bit embarrassed to be a virgin into his twenties.

With Beth he hadn't even been embarrassed to cry and admit he'd been so scared as to wet his pants. Part of him felt like a bit of a wuss regarding the incident, though he was sure that doing anything else would have been a bad idea and likely produced a worse outcome. He was convinced that often discretion was the better part of valor, even when it left you feeling like a wuss.

He'd been happy a few weeks back to learn that Beth shared his interest in old movies--Brando, Newman, Guinness and all the other greats. He was delighted to learn that she played a few chords on the guitar, had a great voice, and enjoyed singing the old folk music. More than anything though, he loved realizing yesterday that, after perusing her beautiful body a long, lingering while--enjoying immensely every lovely nook and cranny--the part of her his eyes still enjoyed resting on most was her dazzling light green eyes and the faint smile so often playing around them and her lips. Suddenly her eyes sent a chill down his spine with just a glance and he was sure they would for a long time to come.

"Hey, how's it going?" Tom asked at the door of Mark's cubicle.

"Oh. Ahhh, pretty good, Pops," Mark answered. He'd been too steeped in thought to see Tom walk up.

"Well, you don't *look* so great, dude. I noticed out front that you look kinda rough around the edges."

"Well, I've been pretty busy and not getting quite enough sleep. You've been even busier though, so I sure shouldn't complain. I'll get caught up on my rest this weekend coming up."

"That's good. I haven't checked the schedule. Which days are you off?"

"Sunday and Monday. I take it that both Mom and kid are doing fine."

"Yeah. She called 'bout half an hour ago. The doc had been in and everything's fine. They'll both be ready to come home tomorrow morning. What's been keeping you up nights? You and Beth having problems."

It was just like Tom. As busy and frantic as his life must be, he was worried about Mark.

"Just the opposite, actually. Our relationship has moved into a new phase. Man it's really hot."

"Oh. You're getting serious. Sounds pretty exciting. Ah to be young and single again."

"Sure, old man. Regret is what you get for robbing the cradle and starting so early. I can't see you being too regretful. Not the way you married so far up. And now with four beautiful kids too."

"Yeah. You know as beautiful as the girls are and as much as I love 'em to death, it's nice looking forward to having a boy to teach baseball to and do things with.

"Say, I read your note on the board about the parking lot. When'd you see this stranger?"

"Yesterday morning. I was out in the lot looking for my wallet. I dropped it in the parking lot Wednesday night when I closed and Dave found it when he came in and left it here on my desk. The stranger didn't look like a hunter or anything. He wasn't close enough for me to get a good look, but I didn't like his body language. Of course I could be wrong, but I pegged him for vagrant ne'er-do-well type.

"What do you think about all employees parking at the other end of the back row? Between bums, skunks and black bears nosing 'round that dumpster, it isn't the safest place, particularly at night. Even though we keep it locked, animals still smell it and come poking around sometimes. In fact I was thinkin' we might want to cordon off an area around it. Keep anyone from parking there. It wouldn't be good to have a customer eaten by any black bear."

"Yeah. Good thinkin', Mark. We can't afford to lose customers. Especially that way." he laughed. "Definitely bad publicity. Let's get on that today. Probably a light out there would be the best idea. Shouldn' cost too much. I'll put that idea in a memo to the regional manager."

"Say, have you let Will in on the good news yet?" Mark asked.

"I talked to him yesterday, while she was in labor. Let's see, what time is it over there? Ah, it doesn't matter. I'll take him at his word. He said to call him any time with the news. We'll get him on Skype while we eat lunch."

Will was Mark's older brother. He and Tom had been best friends since they partnered up on the tennis team their sophomore year at Lincoln High. They were three years ahead of Mark at Lincoln. Will was the brains in the Kwapich family--currently working on his PhD at Freiburg University in Germany. Mark was saving up to go visit him in September.

Mark felt a bit badly about not telling Tom of the incident. It wasn't that he didn't trust Tom. He trusted him totally, but if Mark asked him not to tell anyone else, he knew it would put Tom in a tight spot, because he was supposed to tell the regional manager about any such incidents. Anything untoward that happened on company property was to be reported. Besides, Mark just wanted to put it all behind him as quickly as possible. He'd done the responsible thing. They would increase security around the dumpster and that's most likely all that would be done, whether he reported it or not.

He called Beth. She'd be out of class by now.

"Hi, Mark. How's work going?"

"Not bad. Tom's wife had a boy, so it's a party day. How are you doing?"

"I'm glad to hear it was a boy. Tell him congrats from me. I'm doing pretty good. Berlundre's lecture was even more boring than usual, which I didn't think was possible, but somehow I managed to stay awake."

"Well there's something to be said for staying awake. You know, I'll be off work Sunday an' Monday. I'm thinking about getting away. What I need is a week or two of vacation, but two days 'll have to do. Can you get away?"

"Sorry. Sunday's clear but, much as I'd like, I can't miss Monday classes. I'm afraid I'd even need to take a book along on Sunday. Exams are getting kinda close."

"Okay, so let's get going early Sunday. Just throw a dart at the map and head out at dawn."

"Sure. I'll try to get enough studying done tomorrow while you work."

"Great. What about tonight? I'll be off at eight."

"Gee, those ten hour days are something."

"Yeah, but I do like four day weeks. I may get off a smidgen earlier if all the help shows and we aren't too busy. I'll call you when I leave here, then swing by and we'll pick a place to eat, okay?"

"Sounds good. I'm kinda tired of pizza though. See ya then."

"Sure. Much as I like it, I'm tired of pizza myself. We can do better than that on Friday night. Love ya."

"Love ya too, Mark."

It was another first. The first time they signed off a call like that. It came easily. He felt a butterfly in his stomach.  {~ 3 ~}

## ~ 4 ~

## BEGIN THE TRIP

Mark was glad that Tom took his concern about the dumpster seriously. After the lunch rush he sent a busboy to the hardware store with a list of supplies, then together they marked off a no parking area.

Over their fish dinner he and Beth planned out Sunday's trip.

"Let's draw a random direction," Beth suggested.

So they did just that. With his new expensive pen tingling his fingers just a little, Mark wrote north, east, south and west on four pieces of paper. Then he threw them into the air, having explained, "Any direction that lands face down is eliminated." The only one that landed face up was west.

"I guess west it is," Mark said. "Highway 72. Right past the Daze. You know I've lived around here all my life and never gone very far out that way."

"Go west, young man, go west," Beth agreed. "Shall we take a picnic basket along?"

"Let's just take a few snacks and a jug of lemonade. We'll drive 'til noon, then eat lunch in some small-town diner and find out what's in the area to see and do. We'll take bathing suits and most likely find a place to swim. There's quite a few lakes out that way if I remember correctly."

"Oh that sounds so nice. I can't wait."

"You just study your pretty little head off tomorrow, girl, while I'm working my head off at the Daze and we'll both deserve a one day Sunday vacation. Headless, but other than that ready."

"Kinda gruesome actually. Maybe you should work on some more cheerful metaphors mister creative writer."

"Okay. Maybe I will. I'll make that one of my projects for Sunday. With a notebook and my new magic pen in hand, I'll sit around the beach creating cheerful metaphors to use in my stories."

"Did you say *one* of your projects for Sunday? Pray tell what other projects might you have up your sleeve for our big one day Sunday vacation?"

"We'll see. There may be a surprise or two but then again there may not."

"Oh. Might these surprises involve your *other* magic pen?"

"Oh. Have we started on the metaphors already? I thought I was the creative writer of this group."

"I was just showing how positive they can be. You sure sidestepped the question mister creative writer."

"Yep. I can dance around question with the best of 'em."

"You should be a big time politician or maybe on Dancing with the Stars."

"Maybe I will be on Dancing with the Stars someday when I'm a star. But I'm not sure the show will last that long. It might take me quite a while. So long in fact, that

I may no longer be able to dance. But if that show and I are both viable someday, who knows?"

During dinner, Mark had been thinking about broaching the subject of them renting an apartment together, but he put it off. It would be a Sunday surprise. He might even propose marriage. He felt sure there was nothing he'd like more than to marry her, but maybe it was too fast for Beth. He'd have to think on it.

They slept at his place Saturday night and woke to a beautiful sunrise. As planned, they hurried to get an early start. They each brought a favorite CD, Mark put her guitar in the back seat and Beth put in the small cooler they'd packed the night before. She left her books at home, having studied enough to feel comfortable leaving them behind. They grabbed breakfast at the McDonalds drive-through on their way out of town.

"Actually going west is a great idea. The sun's behind us." Mark observed between bites as he turned onto Highway 72. He tilted his mirrors up so they didn't reflect the sun into his eyes. He didn't slow even an iota passing the Daze.

Beth won the coin toss, so her John Prine CD went in first. They owned the road. He set the cruise control a couple miles over the limit and they sailed through the fresh morning air, booming right along, as Huck Finn would say on the Mississippi.

They discussed John Prine's songs, then the Leonard Cohen songs on Mark's CD which so didn't suit the mood of the occasion that in a strange way they did. He liked "Bird on a Wire" best. She liked "So Long Marianne". They both enjoyed "Susanne" though they equally couldn't figure it out.

"Did you know Cohen wrote novels?" Mark offered.

"Really? I hope they're easier to understand than his songs."

"A friend suggested I read his *Beautiful Losers*.

"Didn't they make a movie of that?" Beth recalled, "It seems to me there was a movie by that name."

"I don't know. We can Google it. If they did, they probably botched it. They usually do."

"But they don't always botch the movie." Beth offered, "What about *The Grapes of Wrath?*."

"Ah, so you've seen that one. It's the exception that proves the rule. I think both the book and movie were off the charts. Script writers stuck to the book. Casting Fonda and Carradine was pure genius.

"How about *One Flew over The Cuckoo's nest?*" Beth asked, "I have thoughts on it, but what do you think?"

"Great book, pretty good movie. Sticking closer to the book would have made a better movie."

"Totally. It wasn't quite a bad movie," Beth said. "Nicholson was such a name, they just made it about him. Kesey wrote it complex with two strong characters. They pretty much simplified it to one.

"My cousin who saw the play in San Francisco said it was closer to the book and better than the movie. Johnny Weissmuller's son played the Indian role."

"Ah yes, Johnny Weissmuller, the real Tarzan. I didn't know he had a son who acted." Mark said. "Did you know they used a recording of his Tarzan yell for several actors who played Tarzan after him?"

"Yeah I read about that," Beth said. "He was a great swimmer. Won freestyle gold medals in the Olympics before becoming an actor. And he did it swimming with his head out of the water, just like he swam as Tarzan."

"Wow. Makes you wonder how fast he would have been if he'd done it right."

"But speaking of great movies, how about *Jaws*?"

"Yeah," Mark said. "Great writing *and* cast."

"Yeah," Beth agreed. "Amazingly great casting. Did you know Shaw was also a widely read novelist?"

"Yeah. He was a villain in an early Bond movie with Sean Connery, too."

"Ah yes. *The* James Bond. You know I saw a great movie last year. Did you see *Searching for Sugarman*?"

"No. I missed it. What's it about?" Mark asked.

"Sixto Rodriguez, a singer-songwriter from Detroit. It won an Oscar for best documentary. You'll enjoy it more if I don't tell you about it. I'd like to see it again."

"Sounds good. That should be fun. I know a really good book I bet you haven't read."

"Oh, what's that?" Beth asked.

*"The Man Who Left Well Enough"*.

"No. Can't say I heard of it. Who wrote it?"

"An Australian fellow I think. Can't remember his name right now. It's the funniest book ever. I have a dog-eared copy I'll loan you."

"What's it about?" Beth asked.

"It's hard to describe. The funniest part is about knicker twangs."

"Knicker twangs?"

"Sure. Grab the wheel. I'll show you."

While Beth held the steering wheel, Mark put his hand under her skirt, pulled the elastic of her undies and let it snap back.

"There, wasn't that exciting?" he asked, retaking the wheel.

"Not too." Beth laughed, "Was it supposed to be?"

"Absolutely. When you read the book, you'll see how exciting knicker twangs can be."

"Okay. I can hardly wait." She laughed. "I read an e-book a while back you'll like--*Love Is The Smile*."

"Tell me about it."

"Oh, it's written by a poet about sex."

"*About* sex."

"Yeah. Mostly about the adventure game," Beth explained. "It's sexy enough to hold you guys' attention and classy enough not to turn us girls off. But it's surprisingly informative. Particularly considering how much we all think we know about the subject. That reminds me, do you like pineapple?"

"Sure. Doesn't everybody? But how does the book remind you to ask me that?" Mark asked.

"Uhhh, welllll, you'll just have to read the book."

"Okay. It's another thing for my to do list. Speaking of food, it's eleven. There aren't any homey little diners on this highway, so it's time we stopped to ask about some such place in the area."

A gas station and souvenir shop came up soon. There they learned of a town about twenty miles north. As they walked out, ice cream cones in hand, Mark had a puzzled look on his face.

"You know, I'm dead certain I've never met that guy in there before, but his voice sounded awfully familiar."

Beth laughed out loud. "Sure. I noticed it right away. It took me a minute to figure out who it was."

"Well, who the heck was it?"

"I can't believe you didn't recognize Dustin Hoffman."

"Oh my gosh, *yes*. It was *him*, wasn't it?" Mark chuckled. "I don't remember ever meeting anyone with such a recognizable voice like that before." Then he recalled recently hearing a voice so like Peter Lorre and he shivered a little.

"It reminds me of when I was a kid. A neighbor across the street looked like Jimmy Carter," Beth said as they got into the car. "The old guy even sounded a bit like Carter. He was nice. All the kids liked him 'cause he gave out big chocolate bars every Halloween. We all called him Mr. Wonka, after Willie Wonka. He got a big kick out of it."

The road they took north was two lane blacktop. It gently curved between tree covered hills that made the air cooler than it had been on the highway. There was an occasional mailbox by a driveway, but no houses visible. Soon the blacktop gave way to gravel. Trees reached out over the road, sometimes nearly touching in the middle. Finally they burst out of the trees, rolled down a hill and into Johnsonville.   {~ 4 ~}

## ~ 5 ~

## SHRUGG, 1 MILE

"Wow. I think we've found Smalltown USA." Beth concluded, viewing a handful of picturesque little pastel houses with flower garden front yards that gave way to a main street of shops suggesting the Civil War era.

"Yeah. It's hard to believe this place exists so near our world, isn't it? Did we step back in time or what?"

They half expected to see horses, buggies and people in eighteenth century garb, but the few vehicles about were motorized, and aged only a few years more than most of those they were accustomed to. The clothing was a few years outdated too. Tony at Tony's Coney Dogs told them about it all.

"Yer a couple o' weeks early fer the horses an' buggies an' ol' fashion clothes an' such. We're gettin' ready fer the founders' day celebration an' the movie folk. Weekend after next, lots o' Amish 'll be in town with their horses an' buggies an' everyone around 'll be decked out like the Civil War was just ended. Then fer two weeks after the celebration them movie folks 'll be all around town shootin' a Civil War movie. They may even be here longer if we're lucky. We're all excited 'bout seein' some real movie stars an' makin' extra money sellin' lots o' extra coney dogs an' souvenirs an' such."

"So you don't do this every year?" Mark asked.

"No. Most years it ain't such a big deal. Jest a bit of a party and all. It's jest every ten years we do it up big and have a real wing ding. We're doin' it up even bigger than big this year on account o' the movie folk."

"Well, we're looking for a place to go swimming this afternoon." Mark said." Is there a lake around here with a public beach where we could swim?"

"Most the folk around here go out North Highway to Whoopsie Lake. It's got a real nice beach. Ain't strictly public for strangers, but most likely ya won't be bothered. If they don't let ya in, jest go on up another mile 'r so ta Jones Lake where there's a private beach. They'll charge ya few bucks, but there ya can swim buck neckked if you want. Bein' young an' city folk I spose ya might. Don't mind admittin' I git up there myself 'bout once each summer. It's a nice place."

They finished two of the best Coney dogs ever, got the directions to Whoopsie Lake from Tony, thanked him with a generous tip and headed north out of town.

"So much for authentic Americana," Mark said. "It's all a big show for the movie folk."

"Oh, I imagine it's pretty good the other nine years between the real wing dings." Beth suggested, "We just showed up the wrong year to be looking for authenticity,".

Two uphill miles from Johnsonville they found North Highway and turned right per Tony's directions.

"Now we just go a piece and there's a sign to Whoopsie Lake. How far do you suppose a piece is according to Tony?" Mark asked.

Beth chuckled. "Well there's a fur piece and a short piece, but all Tony said was a piece, so your guess is as good as mine. The locals go out there to swim though, so I suspect it's no more than a short piece."

A short piece on North Highway became a long piece and then became an even longer piece. Like Highway 72, it was hotter than the cool valley had been.

"We've gone more than a piece, Mark. Do you suppose we've missed it?"

"Well, we've been looking close for the Whoopsie Lake sign. Can't see how we could have missed that. Have you noticed how we've been on this highway nearly an hour and not only haven't we seen a sign for Whoopsie Lake, we haven't seen a sign of *any* kind. No road signs, no billboards, not even a speed limit sign."

"Wait a minute." Beth announced. "I think I see one there ahead."

Mark slowed and stopped at the old faded wooden sign. It read: "Northtown, 3 miles."

"Good." Mark sighed. "I'm sure in Northtown someone can direct us. If we don't reach that lake soon, we'll have no time to swim before we have to head back."

As he passed the sign, it occurred to him that they hadn't yet seen another car going either way, east or west, on this road. No crossroads that he could recall either for that matter. What kind of a crazy road was this? He was relieved that a town was just ahead where they could get information and some gas.

But three miles on he didn't see Northtown, just another faded wooden sign. He stopped on the shoulder by this one and read "Northtown 10 miles." And that's when the car's engine decided to conk out.

"Oh great. Somehow, somebody painted three on that last sign instead of thirteen," Mark surmised, "so now we have ten more miles to go."

He looked over and saw he was talking to himself. Beth had tilted her seat back and fallen asleep.

Good. Let her sleep a while. He'd allow the car to rest a minute and it would likely start. There was still a third of a tank of gas. He, on the other hand, had a full tank in need of emptying. He wasn't comfortable relieving himself in public, even if he hadn't seen a soul for many miles, so he walked through knee high grass to the tree line fifty feet from the road. It was a thick woods except for a gap in front of him where apparently a long unused, barely discernable driveway went into the woods. He walked a few feet on the overgrown driveway and relieved himself.

As he zipped up, he noticed a sign farther along. He walked on to read it. His eyes adjusted to the near darkness as he walked. Approaching the faded sign, he saw that it stood at the beginning of a nicely paved new driveway.

The blacktop approached the highway, then ended about a hundred feet short of it, as though whoever built it had been unable to get a permit to continue it across the county easement and connect it to the highway.

He had to get close to read the sign. It was wooden, similar to the one by the highway, hard to make out in the forest shadows. Finally he read: Shrugg, 1 Mile.

Mark staggered back as though punched in the chest. He spun and ran back toward the car. Suddenly he slowed. *No need to panic. Nothing's happened. Don't scare Beth.*

She was still asleep. He slid into the driver's seat and tried the ignition to no avail. The battery seemed okay, but it wouldn't turn over. It was time to call 911. He pulled out his cell phone and it said no service. *Oh boy.*

Mark sat trying to be calm and gather his thoughts. He pulled the pen from his pocket and stared at the words "Shrugg Inn." He tried to connect the dots. How could the strange man/thing by the dumpster be connected to this place? Could it all be a huge coincidence? Might the train track the guy was following have gone through this town where he just happened to pick up the pen? Or did he perhaps live in this little town? Not quite an impossible coincidence, but throw in this strange road, the weird pen, and that fellow's unbelievable physique, and it was enough to muddle his mind completely.

Mark looked from the pen to Beth's serene face and back to the pen. His eyes went back and forth several times. The vision of that inexplicable seven foot figure by the dumpster lumbered through his mind. He finally tore a page from his writing pad and wrote a note*: Beth, The car won't start and I'm going for help. When you read this try to start the car, then call me on your cell phone. Besides the lemonade in the cooler, there's drinkable water in the windshield washer reservoir. Put our McDonalds straws together to suck it up if you need to. Don't touch the radiator. It has antifreeze. I love you very much. See you soon. Mark.*

He put all the windows down three inches. Mark suppressed a strong urge to kiss Beth on the cheek. He didn't want to risk waking her. He placed the note on the driver's seat, stepped out and headed for Shrugg. It had to be the right decision. He could walk a mile in about fifteen minutes through the cool forest, with no need for water. The highway signs were so screwy that he wasn't sure how far it was to Northtown. If it was a ten mile walk down the hot road, he'd need fluids to have any chance of making it, and he couldn't take any lemonade or water away from Beth.

The blacktop was a bit spongy. His first step on it took him back to the fancy new track he'd run on his senior year of high school. He wanted to think about that regional track meet as he began walking--anything to take his mind off this situation. But his thoughts were as attached to this road as were his shoes. He'd like to run but had to walk. No sense breaking a sweat and wasting body fluid. He didn't know when he'd get water. Shrugg was probably an old railroad town, maybe even just a stop with only two or three buildings. Likely this road was built to transport goods to and from the railroad. The road was quite new, so it seemed there'd be someone there. If it was a sizable town, no doubt a bigger road came in from a different direction for regular traffic.

The road went arrow straight, with trees from both sides crowding in and reaching over to touch each other and form a canopy that cooled his walk. Ten minutes in, the road crossed a bridge over a small stream. Mark clambered down and drank deeply of the cool, sparkling clear water.

Back on the road, he picked up his pace. Beth might wake soon and be frightened. He realized the no service he got when he tried 911 meant her attempt to call him would be fruitless. He'd tried to think of everything but his brain had been addled. Maybe he should have wakened Beth and brought her along. And he should have told her of this road in the note. She'd assume he headed east toward Northtown and go that way if she left the car. He hoped she would stay in the car, but if she thought he headed toward Northtown with nothing to drink, she might take all the water and lemonade she could carry and head out to rescue him. He checked the time on his cell phone. In the note he should have put an estimated time for his return. Damn. What was he thinking?

Far ahead he saw sunshine and broke into a trot. He was back running high school track. The blacktop beneath his feet ended twenty feet before he burst out of the forest into the bright sunshine and Shrugg.   {~ 5 ~}

## ~ 6 ~

# TREED IN SHRUGG

Mark kept running when he emerged from the trees. His eyes adjusted quickly to the brightness, and he ran between houses, old but well-kept and apparently lived in, yet nobody was about. He ran looking for someone to help him so he could quickly get back to Beth. There was nobody on the streets. Actually there were no streets. Just grass. The houses were spaced as though there were streets, but there were none and there weren't any sidewalks either. Just beautiful neat grass everywhere that looked as though every blade had been meticulously mowed yesterday. Where were the people? There had to be somebody around. He needed help. Who the hell mowed the grass for Pete's sake? Was this whole damned town some kind of a house museum or something? Would he have to wait 'til next week when the groundskeeper returned to mow the grass to get help? He'd go back to get Beth, and they could do that he supposed. There was water in the stream that ran under the road and behind most of the houses there were vegetable gardens. They wouldn't starve.

Mark ran out onto the town square beginning to yell for help. His mind was on overload. He wanted to go around and inspect the buildings and figure out what this place was, but he had to find somebody or decide that there was nobody to find and hurry back for Beth. The square was fifty yards across with a handful of trees in the middle. It seemed quite precisely square, with buildings on each side. Those with big front windows had tinted glass he couldn't see through. The doors he tried were locked.

It was time to hurry back for Beth. Everything was locked and no one had responded to his yells. Either nobody was here or everybody was hiding. It suddenly occurred to him that the place must be closed on Sunday. Maybe a school of some sort. He'd get Beth, bring her here, and they'd stay 'til help arrived.

Wait a minute. Which way was the road he came in on? He'd been running around like a chicken with its head cut off and now he didn't know which way to go to find the road. What an idiot. Let's see. Don't panic. They were going east on North Highway and the road into the woods had gone off to the south, so it had to come into Shrugg from the north. Probably near the middle, since there'd been houses either way he looked. So which way was north? Damn. Who could tell? The sun that seemed so bright when he came out of the forest was actually hidden behind a thin haze of clouds. He absently pulled out his phone to check the time. It said one minute later than the last time he'd checked it back on the road. Now the time on his cell phone wasn't even working right. It usually functioned even when he wasn't getting a phone signal. Great. So if the clouds cleared long enough for him to spot a shadow, he'd have to guess the time of day to figure out which way was north.

Enough! It was time to get going back to Beth. It was time to head for the edge of town and walk the tree line around 'til he found the road. Shrugg was a small town. The perimeter couldn't be that big. Mark began jogging directly away from the middle of town through the several rows of houses. From the corner of his eye he glimpsed a movement. He stopped and quickly turned his head. In the house he was passing, a curtain in the window was still moving. It was a closed window.

Mark took the steps to the porch two at a time and pounded loudly on the door. No answer. What was wrong with these people? Wait, he had to calm down. He took a deep breath. Maybe they were timid and afraid of him. They might be deeply religious and spending Sunday indoors praying. Maybe they were afraid of all outsiders. They might shoot him in self-defense if he acted like a crazy man.

Mark tested the doorknob. It turned easily and the door swung wide.

"Hello. Is there anybody here?" He called out in the most soothing friendly voice he could muster. "My car broke down on North Highway and I need a little help."

He stepped hesitantly inside. It was cool, humid and dark except for green lights scattered about, two feet above eye level.

"My girlfriend is waiting for me at the car. I need to get help and go back to her." Whoever it was may not understand English, but they must hear the friendliness and the need in his voice.

He took a tentative step inside and the door swung slowly shut as if closed by a gentle hand. Mark's eyes tried to adjust, but the glowing green lights threw almost no light. He didn't feel alone. He could sense slight movements in what seemed to be a large room. Then came faint rustling, felt as much as heard, and finally light from an indiscernible source filled the room--soft light, just bright enough to show he stood ten feet from five creatures with the unbelievable body build he'd seen only once, walking away from him toward the dumpster.

But they were *not* faceless. No Clint Eastwood hat brims shadowed their faces--startling faces that resembled raccoons with large orange eyes.

Mark stared at them two long seconds and they at him, then the creatures bared their teeth in unison, began emitting high pitched squeals, and moved toward him.

He yanked the door open, and was outside in a bound. One stride on the porch and he flew down the steps touching none. He very nearly pitched forward and fell on his face but, flailing his arms, managed to stay on his feet and ran madly until he reached a large tree in the town square and climbed it with the speed of a monkey. He went as high as the limbs stayed thick enough to hold his weight. There the dense foliage seemed to hide him. He could see nothing through the leaves, so likely the creatures couldn't see him.

During his mad dash, Mark had managed to glimpse back twice and see that they weren't following, so they hadn't seen him climb the tree and he felt fairly safe. They knew he was in Shrugg now though and they'd be looking for him. Under cover of darkness, he'd slip into the woods tonight and in the morning find the road back to Beth who thankfully wasn't here. He was worried about her, but she had enough liquids whether she stayed at the car even a few days, or walked to Northtown. If she walked, he hoped she'd set out in the early morning so there'd be no chance of her being stuck out on the road after dark. He shuddered to think of her out on that road at night. He'd hate to be in that situation himself, especially with these creatures about.

If anyone was looking for him, they weren't making any noise. Perhaps they'd only wanted to shoo him away and thought they'd done so. He unbuckled his belt, pressed himself to the branch and belted himself to it. For once he was glad he had such trouble finding belts short enough for his narrow waist. He often got them as short as possible and then punched a few more holes. Now he needn't fear falling if he slept. He was glad the thick foliage so totally blocked his vision, but the swaying was making him a bit queasy. He hoped the wind didn't pick up. If it did, his vomit might reveal his hiding place.

Mark had time on his hands until dark--time to think and worry about Beth; time to think and worry about the creatures; time to think and worry about how to climb down safely after dark and make an escape. Lots of time to think and worry. His mind flitted back and forth, back and forth like a shuttle-cock in a badminton match 'til he finally dozed off and then awoke in the dark.

It wasn't a quiet darkness though. The night about him was filled with the jabbering squeals of the creatures. None of them seemed up-in-the-tree close, but it was hard to tell how near or far away they were below him. Damn. The huge orange eyes. Of *course* they were nocturnal. That's why they'd all been inside their houses when he arrived. They could most certainly see him better at night than during the day. His escape would need to wait 'til they were sleeping in the broad daylight.

Unbuckling his belt, Mark began to work his way down the limb. He descended carefully, feeling with his feet for small branches to quietly and cautiously ease his weight onto. It was tedious and scary in the dark, but soon he was low enough to see about the square through sparse foliage. He hugged the large limb to remain unnoticed.

From what little he could make out by the moonlight, it looked like a party. It *sounded* like a party too--lots of high pitched jabbering squeals. At least a hundred of the creatures were congregating in the town square near the buildings making those noises, and milling about beneath green glowing globes on the fronts of the buildings. They were staying far from the trees in the center of the square. Mark was happy they didn't spend the night swinging through the trees or his hideout wouldn't have been a secret for two minutes.

Slowly and quietly he slid down the tree, and relieved himself standing tight against the trunk. Had the squeals grown louder, or did they just seem louder from down here? Then, just as slowly and quietly, he shinnied back up the trunk, climbing nearly as high as he had before. Belted back to the limb, he heard the party noise gradually decrease as he drifted into a dreamless sleep.

Dawn was breaking when Mark awoke. He stretched. His muscles ached, feeling every minute of the hours he'd been treed. It was light enough to see that the party was over and the square was deserted. He reached around the branch to unbuckle his belt. That's when he heard Morgan Freeman behind him say softly, "Good morning, Mark. You shouldn't unfasten that belt quite yet." {~ 6 ~}

## ~ 7 ~

## MEET MAGOO

Mark froze. He wanted to run, but it wasn't an option. He faced forward as though there was a gun to his back, his hands hugging the tree, his eyes clenched shut.

"W-w-why? Why shouldn't I unfasten the belt?"

"Because you're surprised and you might fall, Mark. It's a long way down. A fall from this height wouldn't be good. You would be hurt, perhaps even killed."

Mark said nothing. A hundred frenzied questions rushed through his mind, but they fought like a mob of Black Friday shoppers, none making it to his mouth.

After a moment Morgan spoke. "You can turn your head around now, Mark. I promise I won't hurt you."

He opened his eyes, slowly turned his head and saw a visitor perched in the next branch over. But for his face, he looked like those creatures. The face, however, was the spitting image of Mr. Magoo. Mark nearly laughed.

"See? I told you I'd surprise you." Magoo grinned. "Aren't you glad I didn't wait 'til your belt was loose?"

"Who the heck are you? Are you one of those creatures? How come you speak English?" Mark asked in machine gun run-on-sentence form, while unable to refrain from reflecting Magoo's infectious smile.

"Okay, okay hold on. One answer at a time. First of all I don't have a name in your language. If I could still say it in my language, it would sound like a bunch of squeaks to you. I can't say it though, because my vocal chords have been altered to allow me to speak English. So if you'd like to name me in English, feel free to do so any time.

After a rather lengthy hesitation, Mark offered slowly, "How about Morgan Magoo? You certainly sound like Morgan Freeman and totally look like Mr. Magoo."

"Why didn't I think of that?" Magoo laughed. "Very good, I'm Morgan Magoo."

"Now, Mark, before we get started, there's something I seriously must do. I must ease your mind about the thing most important to you. Don't worry about your girlfriend, Beth. She's fine. You'll return to your car, and when you do, she'll be safely asleep in the front seat. If you stay here a few days, she'll have slept only hours, because time goes differently in Shrugg. So there's no need for you to worry about her while you're here."

Mark felt a flood of relief as Magoo talked. For some reason the old guy sounded so trustworthy that Mark believed his every word.

"Next, I owe you a couple of apologies. But there's no hurry for them. Did you know there's food at the bottom of this tree?" Magoo was whispering and pointing down with a childish grin and twinkle in his eye. "I'd love to sit up here all day, but you'd be more comfortable down there, and I think we're both pretty hungry.

"Oh, but there's one thing I need to tell you before we go down, Mark. Everybody's at home asleep. So there's nobody around and you can run faster than me or any of us. That means you can escape into the woods whenever you want, but you won't find the road until I show you where it is. So we would just have to follow you until you got tired of wandering around in the woods and decided to come back here with us. That would all just be a big waste of time.

"Now let's go down and eat, and then I'll make my apologies and try to answer all your questions. Be careful now. Go slowly. My friends tell me you're as extremely clumsy as expected up here, and I'm not strong enough to help you much or keep you from falling."

Mark unbuckled his belt and they climbed down, both very slowly, though Mark sensed that Magoo could have descended far more quickly. He moved through the tree with a relaxed ease that Mark had to admit did make him look extremely clumsy.

The food was two big bowls of salad full of fresh vegetables, each with a large glass of cold water beside it. The bowls rested on a small round pink table with two chairs, both with a full complement of silverware.

As he stepped onto the ground, Magoo said, "I know this isn't your usual breakfast, but I hope it will do.

"I'm sure you're quite as hungry as me, but we should step over into that building and use the lavatory first, don't you think?"

"Of course," Mark agreed. He was taking in the sight of Magoo. It was his first look at one of the creatures in daylight. Magoo was nearly seven feet tall with a build rather like SpongeBob on stilts, just like the back he'd last seen walking toward the dumpster. He was dressed all in the brown of a boy scout, with no shoes. His trunk was perhaps a little wider than it was high and the four-foot-long arms were there too. The only thing he lacked was the large shoulders. Mark suspected that Magoo, with a pair of shoulder pads, might have been his mugger.

Mark found the restroom amazingly clean and modern. He spent little time scrutinizing it, though. Both being ravenously hungry, they were back at the table in record time.

They didn't speak while they ate the feast of tomatoes, greens, mushrooms and a few other vegetables he didn't recognize. Mark was accustomed to dressing on his salad, but hungry enough to eat nearly anything. These, however, were the most delicious vegetables he'd ever eaten--each perfectly ripe, very juicy and a treat to excite the taste buds. The water was sparkling clear and icy cold.

When they'd finished, Magoo said, "Now, Mark, I want you to understand that I deeply regret the way our first meeting went. That was me you met a few nights back in the parking lot. I was quite scared. Perhaps as scared as you, because you're much stronger than I am and faster too. I was afraid that if you didn't fear me you might do me bodily harm. Perhaps I went a little overboard on the scare tactics. I really had no knife and hoped you'd just give me a little money and I'd give you the pen. As scary as I tried to look, wearing shoulder pads and all, you didn't offer me anything, so from there on I had to wing it. I'm sorry. I owe you a favor someday for doing such a terrible thing. Please accept my apology for scaring you so."

"Apology accepted, Magoo. I understand. It was partly my fault. I was foolish for not giving you a buck or two in the first place. I don't know what I was thinking. It all happened so fast. I just wasn't ready. I think I must have figured that if I pulled my wallet out you would grab it. Anyway, I was the most scared I've ever been in my life, but I'm over it now. You needn't owe me a favor."

"Oh, but I very definitely do. It's absolutely our custom that when one wrongs somebody, that person is then owed a favor of equal or greater value in return."

"Well, you've eased my great worry about the safety of my loved one, Beth, and I consider that a most wonderful favor."

"No. that was a common courtesy and it won't do. Your time spent carrying such great worry about her was also our fault so, if anything, I owe you two favors.

"Now, I'm also sorry I wasn't here to greet you when you arrived. Some slight misadventures on my return trip delayed me, and you arrived a bit more quickly than expected. That family didn't know what to do when you woke them. They were quite afraid of you at first--afraid you would hurt them. So they tried to scare you off. They weren't trying to hurt you, Mark. We're nearly always very timid and friendly and I promise that you needn't worry about anyone hurting you while you're here.

"So I've made my apologies and perhaps answered some of your questions, but I know you have many more. Ask me whatever you like and I'll do my best to answer your every question."

Mark thought for a moment, sorting out which question to ask first, "Where are you crea…ahhh, people from, and how did you get here?"

"Oh, we're from a planet very far away that's quite similar to Earth, and we came on what you would call a large spaceship. It looks more like a glass ball though, the kind you shake and make the snow inside fly around.

"You see our star was failing badly, giving off less and less light and heat, so we had to escape before it imploded. Ours was one of a thousand ships sent out, each to a different planet."

"How long did your trip take?"

"Well, time is a funny thing, Mark. There were about three hundred and fifty of us on the ship and we each spent most of our time asleep. Not really asleep. We were actually very near death. Rather like hibernating but even deeper. While we were in that state our bodies didn't age.

"Only three of us were awake at any given time, so it was a relay. We each stayed awake one or two days and then we awoke others before we went back to sleep. Even those days were far shorter than Earth days. So we each aged about twenty years during the trip.

"We started our journey millions of years ago by Earth time and we traveled somewhat faster than the speed of light. We've come quite a distance."

"So how long have you been here?"

"By Earth time, only ten days."

"And you traveled faster than the speed of light?"

"Yes. I know that seems impossible to you. Our technology is different from yours. There is some of yours we haven't yet figured out, and much of ours I'm sure your greatest minds wouldn't comprehend easily."

"But what about you? How is it that you speak English? You even speak it as well as anyone I know. Today you sound just like Morgan Freeman, but the other night you sounded just like Peter Lorre. And you don't look like those other crea…, people around here."

"Well, thank you. I try to speak well, Mark. I'm actually a fairly successful experiment. On our way here I studied your civilization using movies and radio broadcasts. Unfortunately your TV technology still eludes us.

"During the trip my vocal chords were changed to allow me to speak English. So then I learned to speak your language. It's much easier than ours. One must be far smarter to learn our language. I wish the inventor of our language had been smart enough to make it as simple as yours.

"My face too was modified, but less successfully than my vocal chords. There was much trouble with the eyes. I no longer see the green light spectrum I once did, but I don't see too well in the daylight either. It's ironic that I see nearly as poorly as the delightful Mr. Magoo I was made to so resemble. We've postponed further experimental face work 'til we figure out the eyes better. We're working on them. They're most intricately configured.

"I'm getting very sleepy, Mark. I traveled most of last night and arrived back only a few minutes before you awoke. I know you have more questions and I'll try to answer them all after a few hours of sleep. Come, I'll show you where you can stay while you're here."

Magoo did sound exhausted. Mark followed him to a small house. He walked even slower than slow.

"This will be your house while you're in Shrugg. I live right over there. I doubt you slept well in that tree last night, so you may be ready to sleep. If not, you might spend some time writing down some questions for me. I don't think you should go out after dark. They're not used to you yet and they're afraid of you. Another meal will soon be left on your porch. I'll come and wake you when I am rested. I doubt I will sleep 'til dawn, but if you waken and it's light out, you may come wake me."

With that, Magoo turned and lumbered laboriously home.

Mark studied his tired back as he walked so slowly to his home across the way, and wondered about his age. He was certainly no spring chicken. He'd aged twenty years on the trip to Earth. He also said he had some misadventures on his way back to Shrugg. Mark wondered what kind of misadventures an alien with his appearance could have, yet get back home unscathed. No wonder he was tired. It must have taken great courage for him to venture out into a totally strange foreign world alone. He'd been unarmed and known he was slower and weaker than any man he might meet. To top it off, he didn't see very well. And to say he was conspicuous was a sizeable understatement. He'd seemed quite calm all morning, with his droll Morgan Freeman voice, but Mark couldn't see how any misadventures he had could be anything other than unnerving. Magoo had to be quite a trooper to say the very least.

Mark toured his new home. It was very clean, but with a slight musty odor. He opened three of the darkly tinted windows to allow in some sunlight and fresh air. The kitchen was bare but for ice in the freezer, and there were towels, soap and a toothbrush in the bathroom, a few pair of brown pants on the bed, underwear and socks in the dresser and some brown shirts in the closet. The shirts and pants were the same color Magoo wore. Everything looked made to fit Mark. The furniture seemed like a cut rate motel except for the bed. He laid back and sunk right in--it enveloped him cocoon-like. It was most comfortable but climbing out was a struggle.

Tired, yet not really sleepy, Mark did some exercises to stretch his aching muscles. Then he decided to do as Magoo had suggested and write out some questions. Lord knows he had a myriad of them. There was a pad of paper on the coffee table and he had his magic pen. About twenty questions later he realized that he was certain to have many more questions, but those questions would depend on the answers he'd receive.

He heard a tapping on his door and opened it rather quickly, yet not quickly enough to see whoever delivered the food on his porch. The tray held a bowl of salad smaller than the one he enjoyed for breakfast. Beside it was a plate of fish and loaf of bread. Instead of water, there was a large glass of pink wine.

Mark hadn't felt particularly hungry, but the cuisine looked like what he imagined of an exclusive restaurant. The enticing aroma increased his hunger tenfold. One bite savored and he couldn't stop eating. He had to remind himself several times to ingest slowly and allow the celebration of flavors to linger a while on his delirious tongue.

Finished, Mark was comfortably full, yet were there more, he knew he would have been incapable of stopping until he was beyond stuffed. He recalled hearing of bacchanalian feasts where the Romans threw up for the enjoyment of eating more, and he could nearly see himself there.

The large glass of heavenly wine made him so sleepy he could hardly stay awake through brushing his teeth before falling into the comfortable womb-like mattress and a most rejuvenating sleep. {~ 7 ~}`

## ~ 8 ~

## SHRUGG

In the morning Mark again exited the mattress with great difficulty'. The expression "climbed out of bed" was most appropriate. Had he the build of Magoo, he assumed it would be a much lesser task.

The breakfast he found on his porch after he showered and shaved was the usual salad beside a plate of scrambled eggs and a large glass of orange juice. Again it was a delectable treat for the taste buds. If the way to a man's heart was through his stomach, Mark considered these folks definitely headed in that direction.

As he finished breakfast Magoo arrived. Yesterday's great weariness seemed to be history. His step was quicker and his smile was back.

"Good morning, Mark," He answered to Mark's greeting. "You look to have slept and eaten well. Are the accommodations quite suitable?"

"Oh the food is absolutely awesome. I'm eating like a king. Do all the people here eat so well?"

"Oh yes. Though, to be honest, we do tend to eat a bit less. You're getting enough, aren't you? If you need three meals each day, I could see that you get more for breakfast and you could save some in your refrigerator for mid-day."

"I was fine yesterday, thanks. I'll mention it if I feel the need. Oh, and everything else was quite excellent too. Let me ask my first question. How long do you expect my stay in Shrugg to be?"

It was a question Mark had rehearsed, wanting to be as diplomatic as possible with no hint that he realized he was, in fact, a prisoner until Magoo showed him the road out.

"We need you to stay a few days if possible, Mark. You're entirely welcome to stay a week, but after that you must leave. By Earth time, you'll be gone only hours."

"Well, Magoo, if you keep feeding me like a king, you may have trouble chasing me off." Mark laughed. "But seriously, that does seem fair enough. You've certainly gone through a lot of trouble to get me here, though. Why do you need me?"

"Mainly we want you to attend a council meeting. We also wish to study you and perhaps make a clone before you leave. The study will be mostly behavioral psychology stuff. Oh, there'll be some medical tests too, but that'll take only a couple of hours and be absolutely painless."

"A council meeting, medical poking and prodding, a clone and psychological testing. That sounds like a busy few days."

"Somewhat. I'll be with you much of the time though, and whenever I'm not near, you may summon me with this." Magoo said and pulled a beeper from his pocket. It was on a cord which he slipped over Mark's head so it hung like a referee's whistle around his neck. "Don't hesitate. You're my responsibility while you're here. I may take time out to do some other less important things, and I also don't wish to smother you, but I *can* be with you every minute, day and night, if you wish.

"I can tell you about everything but the psychological stuff. If I tell you about that it will skew the observations. Just let me say that if, while you're here, you see something that appears different from what I've told you, don't believe your lying eyes, Mark. Trust what I tell you."

Mark saw that he needed to place an uncomfortable amount of trust in Magoo while he was in Shrugg--trust that all the medical and psychological tests were safe and harmless; trust that in the end he'd be allowed to leave alive and shown the way out; trust that Beth would be well and asleep in the car; now trust in Magoo's words over what he might see with his own eyes. Yet his instincts did say Magoo was trustworthy and there seemed to be no real alternative. He was, in fact, a prisoner who could be forced to do anything he was being asked to do in a friendly way.

"Well, tell me about this committee meeting?"

"The council is our ruling body, Mark. We meet to discuss problems and vote on solutions. There's always much disagreement and arguing at these meetings. I'm one of the thirty voting members. We're eager for your opinions and ideas. They'll be carefully weighed, but you won't vote. Actually, we seldom do vote. Everything gets put off 'til the next meeting.

"It's going to be a bit cumbersome. I'll be your interpreter, but my vocal chords can no longer speak their language, so I'll need to type everything that's said."

"So what problems will be discussed?"

"Oh, some petty stuff. The three important ones that we've been debating forever are population growth, clone problems and Earth problems. You're here to talk about the Earth problems. I don't want to discuss those with you because the council wants unrehearsed answers at the meeting. We want your spontaneous answers."

"I don't feel qualified to…"

"We know you're no expert, Mark. We don't expect you to be. Just be honest."

"Okay. Shouldn't be a problem. So what are your problems with population and clones?"

"Basically we lost a generation while we were traveling. We prepared for this as best we could by bringing many families with young children, as well as some orphans, but those children are in their twenties now. They have lost many of their reproductive years. We were having problems with our fertility rate back home before we left. Recently we learned that several of our younger men are infertile. One way we may solve that problem soon is through multiple births.

"The problems with the clones are complicated, Mark. One problem is that according to our laws, they have all the rights of any other person, except the right to vote. When they're created they're quite perfect duplicates, yet in time they often begin to break down. Sometimes as soon as year after they're created. Other times somewhat later.

"The problem is a moral one. What to do when a clone begins to break down. We have played God and created beings with abilities, knowledge and feelings. Do we have the right to discard them when they're guilty of having faults? One cannot legally kill one's own child for any reason. As our creation, a clone is our child. We even let them keep our name. Their names aren't capitalized though. This differentiates the self from his clone."

"So, what are you doing when they break down?"

"When they're judged dangerous, we put them away and often keep them mildly sedated, while they become an increasing drain on our resources, and we wrestle with the problem.

"Come, bring your list of questions, and let's walk."

And so they went out walking in Shrugg while Magoo answered Mark's questions.

"How did you chose me to bring to Shrugg?" Mark asked.

"That night we had a device to measure brain waves. Yours registered above the level we required, you were sober and you were alone. We didn't wish to confront more than one person or someone who'd been drinking."

"You keep saying *we*. I thought you were alone?"

"No. There was a woman with me behind the waste removal container. She was along to assist me and attempt a rescue if needed. In Shrugg, women, though the same size, are faster, heavier, and nearly twice as strong as men. I must mention, however, men average measurably six percent more intelligent. Anyway, one of our strongest women was with me."

As they entered the square, Mark asked. "Why does Shrugg have trees only in the square? You seemed so at ease in that tree, and yet nobody goes near the trees."

"It was only because you were here, Mark. On any normal night many of us are in those trees. That night they were afraid they would scare you away, so they just sat back and enjoyed watching you. Our planet is quite covered with trees larger and closer together than yours on Earth and we spent most of our time in trees. Here we have trees only in the square so we'll walk more and strengthen our legs."

"So I wasn't hidden. They could see me in the dark?"

"Yes. Those bulbs you saw glowing green, light up this place like daylight for them. It's a light spectrum different from what your eyes, and now mine, can see. They go out in daylight wearing special sunglasses and see fairly well. It helps that we also have a haze dome over Shrugg. It filters out the rays that would severely damage our skin. We'd be more comfortable if the haze filtered out even more of the spectrum, but then all the vegetation would die and we'd starve. We've been most fortunate with our vegetables. Many of the plants we brought are thriving in this sunlight and atmosphere. We worked hard hybridizing them during our trip. Plants that evolved in the green light of our planet wouldn't survive here."

They sat in the town square and Magoo continued to answer questions. Mark occasionally spied one of the creatures out and about wearing big sunglasses.

"Do you notice that they won't stare at you? That would be impolite." Magoo explained. "Don't stare at them. Glance, then look away for a while. Staring at groups a bit is fine. Staring at one alone is very rude."

It wasn't easy, but Mark would work on it.

"Now it's nearly time for dinner." Magoo announced. "I suggest we retire to our homes to eat and rest. I'll come by shortly after dusk and we'll go out a bit so you can see what it's like around here after dark. We can't stay out too late though. Busy day tomorrow. At noon you're scheduled for medical tests. It'll be good to get them out of the way. The council meets in the evening."

*Tomorrow did sound like a busy day*, Mark thought as he sat in his spartan kitchen eating yet another simply delectable meal. The medical tests and council meeting would likely go as smoothly as butter, the way the calm assurance in Magoo's voice clearly implied. That didn't keep Mark from worrying a bit. Were the tests as routine, harmless and noninvasive as Magoo said? And might there be surprises at the council meeting? He could only wait and see.

When Magoo came by after dusk he had night vision glasses. Everything was shades of green, but Mark could see pretty well. Magoo saw even more poorly than he did in daylight. He knew the place like the back of his hand though, so he got around all right.

As they walked toward the square, Mark asked Magoo what his official title was in Shrugg.

"The council is the ruling body and everyone on the council has an equal vote, so I'm no more important than any other council member, though I'm considered the top scientist. I supervise the other scientists, a duty which often bears immense similarity to herding felines."

"Wow. So how is it that you spend so much time with me when you must have so much to do?"

"You're our most important area of research. You're the first earthling we've studied or had contact with. Also a clone is doing some of my work."

"I didn't know I was so important, Magoo. How many scientists do you have?"

"About sixty."

"That's quite a few."

"Yes. Many of them have assistants, too. We have many areas of study."

"Shrugg is so small. Where are your laboratories?"

"Some are on our mother ship buried on the dark side of your moon. That's where we spent years, preparing our landing. It's where I learned English watching drive-in movies. I had trouble with the sound, but then they got rid of the old speakers every one kept driving off with, and put the sound on the radio."

Magoo went on telling Mark about Shrugg, the ship on the moon and the lengthy trip from his homeland.

"This is all so amazing Magoo. How is it that you feel free to give me so much information? Aren't you afraid our government might learn about you from me?"

"Do you think they'd believe you if you told them about us, Mark? If you tell her about us, Beth will surely believe you, yet she can't corroborate your story. You were there when she fell asleep. She's sleeping for just a few hours. And you'll be there when she wakes up."

"Yeah."

"We may contact your government someday, Mark. Perhaps quite soon. That's one thing we've been debating at council. You'll learn about that tomorrow evening."

"Speaking of the meeting, I want your assurance that you'll accurately tell me everything the members of the council say. Whether it's embarrassing, stupid, painful, insulting, whatever, I want it unfiltered. Don't leave out anything for any reason."

"Okay. I'll tell everything as accurately as possible."

"Well your English is certainly good enough--it's better than anybody I know. You've been speaking their language forever too, so you should be really accurate."

"Mark, not every word in each language translates exactly into the other. But don't worry, I won't sugarcoat anything."

"Okay. But tell me how the heck you learned such perfect English all by yourself."

"Oh I watched lots of those drive-in movies, then, when we first arrived here on Earth, I snuck out to a bookstore, hiding myself under a winter overcoat, and managed to purchase a dictionary, a thesaurus, many novels and some grammar books and I memorized them. Then I watched more movies, so now I do pretty well."

Mark and Magoo sat and talked on a bench in the square while they watched the goings on about them. As Magoo had said, climbing in the trees was a popular pastime. So too was a game which appeared very similar to bocce ball, as well as a board game resembling chess with three players playing very slowly on a triangular board. Magoo explained that only a fifth of the population was here any given night. Everyone worked four nights, then had a night off.

Many of the buildings around the square appeared to be either restaurants or bars with creatures going in and out regularly. Their raucous squealing burst out through the open doors. Mark couldn't tell whether everyone inside was laughing, arguing or shouting. Whichever they were doing, they all seemed to be doing it at the same time with great vigor. Magoo said they could go inside one of the better restaurants, but it would be best if they stayed out a few nights until the natives of Shrugg got more used to Mark. That was fine with him. He wasn't too sure he wanted to go inside, though Magoo assured him that they would be well treated and there was excellent food and drink to be had inside.

They retired early and in the morning ate breakfast together at Magoo's. Mark was surprised to find his home was furnished quite similarly to Mark's. Magoo told him that most bachelors had similar accommodations. Magoo's wife had passed away a year before the voyage began. Were she with him, it would look quite different. Mark offered his condolences and asked about his children. Magoo explained that two were scientists back at the ship and his eldest was the lead scientist on another ship destined for another galaxy.

Sensing Mark had some uneasiness about them, Magoo spent much of the morning telling him about the medical tests to which he was about to be subjected. Several of them Magoo had had a hand in designing. In fact, two were entirely of Magoo's creation. He proudly explained those two in great detail.

So when Mark walked into the clinic he was well prepared for the poking and prodding he received; the attaching and reattaching of sensor wires; the treadmill running; the weight lifting and more. Though rather tiring, it all went as smoothly and easily as Magoo had predicted.

Sitting with Magoo on a bench in the deserted town square after the tests Mark asked, "So what's in all this for me, Magoo?"

"What do you mean, Mark?"

"Well, you've been very good to me, Magoo, and I do appreciate that you've treated me very well while I've been here. But first you gave me the worst scare I've ever had in my life, then somehow you brought me here and got all this medical test information from me, and tonight you're going to ask information about Earth from me-- not that I know all that much. Then you're going to do some behavioral psychological studies and finally before you let me go home, you're going to make a clone of me to keep and use for who knows what. Then I'll most likely never see you again. It seems that you get an awful lot from my visit here. What do I get in return?"

Magoo thought for a few seconds. "I guess not a whole lot, Mark. That does remind me of one thing though." He reached into his pocket. "Here are the forty-one dollars that I borrowed from your wallet that night. I've been carrying it around and keep forgetting to give it to you.

"Yes we got you here in an impolite and deceitful manner and I know this episode hasn't been easy for you. Had I the ability to erase it from your memory, I would. It's been no pleasant trip to Disney World, though perhaps you could think of it as a trip to a grown-up's Disney World. You're the first earthling to travel to this dimension, and, as far as I know, the first to meet and communicate with anyone from another world.

"As for tangible rewards, you'll take home only a souvenir pen guaranteed to write smoothly the rest of your life and never leak ink in your pocket. Perhaps I should have it inscribed--I went all the way to Shrugg and all I got was this damned pen." Magoo chuckled.

"I owe you a favor, however, I can think of none to give other than your safe return to Beth asleep in the car. That hardly counts as a favor since your stressful circumstances are of our making.

"There are intangible rewards you might consider taking in return for your trouble, though. You may accept the satisfaction of knowing you've made important contributions to science and to the beginning of communication between our worlds. I expect you and I'll be considered pioneers one day. We'll be a footnote in an important chapter of history which will hopefully improve both our worlds.

"As for your clone, we plan to use it to continue our scientific research. We'll alter its appearance, so it can't be traced to you, then we expect it to enable us to contact individual earthlings more easily. It may also be sent into your world to retrieve items of interest to us.

"Now let's go home to eat and rest. Tonight's council meeting may be long and tiresome. They usually are, and I expect this one to be no different."

The largest building on the square held the meeting hall. Magoo showed Mark around in it before the meeting. There were six round tables with five chairs each in the main hall and six doors to smaller meeting rooms around the hall. The main room and all six smaller rooms were round. Each of the smaller rooms held a round table with five chairs around it. Magoo explained that the smaller rooms were the organizing rooms where groups organized their thoughts. In other words, that's where they argued.

As they filed into the hall, it sounded to Mark as though they were all arguing already. Magoo said no, they were joking around and exchanging pleasantries.

"Are they talking about me?" Mark asked.

"Many are."

"What are they saying?"

"They aren't being particularly respectful, Mark. I know I promised to tell you everything, but I don't think it would be fair for me to tell you what they're saying when they don't think you will understand. These are things they wouldn't say if they thought you would understand. Now I'll warn them that I'm going to tell you everything and then I'll keep my promise and tell you all I can. There are twenty nine of them, however, and they can speak much faster than you."

Magoo pushed a button on the table before him, a loud gong noise sounded, and the room grew quiet as he typed lightning fast on the keyboard before him. The words he typed appeared on a large screen on the wall behind us in their language. His words were met with silence.

"Okay, I've told them of my agreement with you to tell all, and that I will be honoring it from this point on. Now I'm telling them that they must speak slowly and one at a time so that I can interpret for you. I'm also suggesting that we honor you as a guest by going to that business which involves you first, so you needn't stay for the rest of the meeting."

Mark thought he'd like to stay. He was curious about the nature of their clone problems. He realized, however, that those problems were really none of his business, and he also suspected that translating would be a tiresome task for Magoo.

After a rather lengthy silence one member stood and spoke. When he finished, Magoo translated for Mark. "He says they're aware that you're no scientist and they're uncertain what questions to ask. So it would be best if you asked questions to get the conversation started."

Mark hesitated only a couple seconds before saying, "Okay. You made a long voyage to come here and reached Earth very recently. What's your plan now that you're here?"

All the members quickly began talking among themselves.

"What are they saying, Magoo?"

"They're discussing what they should reveal to you. I will speak." He pressed the button for the gong.

They all quieted while Magoo typed a message and then began talking again.

"I told them that you have no friends in your government, so no one there will hear what we say. Nobody there will believe you have been here or that we exist. However, even if there's the slightest chance that's not true, we've nothing we wish to hide from the people of Earth. Quite the contrary. We'd like to meet and be friends with them.

"Now Mark, I'm going to begin typing their answers in English. It will be faster and easier. You just read them on the screen."

Soon a member stood, spoke and Mark read. "Leaving our planet we knew little of Earth. Only that our best scientific data said there was an eighty-three percent chance we would find it habitable. That was good. Most of the ships went to planets where the chances of success were lower. Then we studied this planet during our trip--analyzing every piece of data; getting information more and more accurate as we approached. We got very accurate and most disturbing data while preparing to disembark from your moon.

"Our plan since the beginning was to inhabit Earth, sharing it with whatever forms of life we would find here. We're pilgrims who've come out of necessity from a dying planet. Our ship was designed for a single voyage, so staying on Earth is our only option. So you see our situation.

"Our biggest problem is that from your moon, we watched this planet and its atmosphere deteriorate very quickly as we prepared to land. Earthlings are severely damaging the planet we planned to share with them for a long time. So we're debating what our plan should be. Should we make our presence known and try to help them quit savaging the planet? It would be easier to get rid of them and have the place to ourselves--a safer plan of action for us and one much more certain to save the Earth."

"You would wage war against us?" Mark asked.

"No. We have no experience with war. We've always been peaceable. We would kill you off by peaceful means, something your war on your environment is about to do anyway. The difference is that if we exterminate, it would be more humane and leave a repairable planet for us to inhabit.

"So which direction do you think our plan should take?"

"Well, you seem to be good moral people--people with good intentions. Clearly the moral path for you is to help us save the Earth where we can both live in harmony."

"Earthlings aren't in the habit of being harmonious. You have a history of quarreling in the most disgusting and often immoral ways. Also we've heard about the movies of visitors from outer space--movies full of violence. They seldom end well. Could we safely make contact? I understand that your smallest dogs often bite people out of fear. Could we contact earthlings without being in danger of fear-biting?"

*[handwritten margin note: is this mark? IF so— you need question marks.]*

"It would not be easy to do, but certainly it would be safe for you to communicate from here in a dimension where earthlings can't find you."

"We've learned how to travel between these dimensions. How long would it take earthlings to figure it out?"

Mark said nothing.

"We debate these things here in Shrugg. Our immediate plan is to have one of your top scientists come communicate with us. Could you give us the name of a scientist you would suggest?"

"I'm sorry. I don't know the names of any scientists."

"You don't know the names of *any* scientists?"

"No."

"What kind of people run your countries on Earth?"

"Mostly the richest people and lawyers."

Mark heard squeaky chirping throughout the room which he took for laughter. Magoo typed nothing.

"They're laughing?" He asked Magoo.

"Yes. It's quite rude."

Before Magoo could hit the button to ring the gong and rebuke them, the speaker asked, "Do any other types of people lead your countries?"

"Often military men."

This elicited no laughter--stone silence.

"But no scientists?"

"None that I know of."

"And what about philosophers and poets?"

"No. None of those."

This brought squeaky noise from many of the others. It didn't sound quite like the laughter. Mark turned to Magoo with a questioning look, and Magoo answered. "Some of them are scientists and nearly as many are

76

philosophers or poets. It's a friendly rivalry. They're doing what you call exchanging barbs. Being better with words, the poets always win at that."

Magoo waited a minute before ringing the gong and typing in: *Does anyone else have more questions of our guest?*

Another member stood and asked, "Do you know how we can find a scientist to bring here to talk?"

"I suggest you go to a university science department and find a professor."

"Any university?"

"Well, just don't go to a smaller religious school. There you might find someone who doesn't believe in science."

Mark recognized low laughter rippling among the delegates.

"There are people in your society who do not *believe* in science?"

"Yes."

This brought louder laughter.

Magoo reached for the button to sound the gong, but Mark grabbed his hand.

"Yes, there are quite a few and I too find them quite funny."

"How do these people disprove the work of many generations of scientists? Are your scientist not required to prove their discoveries?"

"Oh yes. Scientific discoveries are published and scrutinized by the entire scientific community. These people don't spend time trying to dis*prove* science, they just decide to dis*believe* it."

The laughter grew louder.

"Certainly these people are laughed at."

"By many, yet they fool enough people to sometimes get voted onto councils."

There was a sudden silence.

"So you have people like this on *council*?"

"Well, we have many councils and some of these people are voted onto them."

"But not your high councils."

"Yes, occasionally even our highest councils."

The silence of the room burst into loud squeals. Everybody babbled at each other. Magoo pressed his button, but the gong went unheard in the mayhem. He shouted in Mark's ear that they should leave, this part of the meeting was over.

"Well, I think that went really well." Mark laughed nervously as they stepped outside.

"You were quite articulate and they recognized that you were being very honest. Those are most important things for you, Mark. So actually it did go quite well. We got some accurate information, and that's what we wanted. Now you go get to bed. This meeting's bound to end late, so I'll sleep most of the morning and see you shortly before noon."

Mark slept late and his breakfast was in the refrigerator. A note on the bathroom mirror told him so. He was uncomfortable that they'd been in his place while he slept. He might mention it to Magoo. Just as some things were impolite in Shrugg, so too were some things impolite for earthlings.

He felt a bit grumpy. He'd had a particularly difficult struggle climbing out of that damned Chinese finger trap of a mattress. The previous morning he thought he was beginning to get the hang of it, but there really didn't seem to be any easy way out--not even a moderately easy way. He wondered what the trick would be if he was seven feet tall with a body like SpongeBob.

While he ate breakfast, Mark ruminated the give-and-take at last night's council meeting. Most alarmingly he'd learned that they were seriously considering annihilating Earth's population and seemed calmly certain they could do so. He'd have to ask Magoo whether they could actually eliminate the people and not harm the Earth. If so, perhaps he could learn *how* they would do it.

He believed they wanted peace. They said they had no experience with war. Yet they were considering a preemptive war that would kill billions of innocent people. But could you blame them? There was clearly sense in their logic and desperation in their situation. Fortunately it appeared that cooler heads would prevail, and they would team up with earthlings to save the Earth.

When Mark finished breakfast and cleaned up after himself a little, he had two hours to kill. He'd go for a walk. He wanted to casually peruse the tree line around Shrugg. He wasn't anxious to leave right away, yet he'd be more comfortable if he knew the way out. Was the road he came in on actually impossible to spot? He doubted Magoo would say that just to keep him from looking, but...

## ~ 9 ~

## MORE HUGGING

It was another beautiful morning. The haze over Shrugg kept the sun's location as well hidden as usual, hence the compass directions unfathomable. Mark hadn't the slightest inkling about which part of town he'd seen first when he arrived. So he just walked to the nearest edge of town, crossed the forty foot lawn area and turned left at the tree line. He remembered that the road stopped short of the tree line though and realized he wouldn't spot it from out here looking into the darkness of the shady forest. So he walked twenty feet into the trees and began following the tree line along inside the forest, being careful not to lose sight of the clearing. His head was on a swivel; keep looking right searching for the road; keep looking left not to lose sight of the clearing. With little underbrush to impede him, it was quite a pleasant trek.

After walking a while, he realized he'd left no marker when he started, so he could circle Shrugg more than once and not know it. Suddenly he heard his name whispered loudly. He turned to his right and twenty feet away beth stepped from behind a tree.

"Quick, Mark! They're not watching! Follow me this way!"

She ran and he followed her. He was trying to catch up to tell her he didn't want to leave yet, but she wasn't slow. The forest floor was smooth with spongy moss and little underbrush. At the Kentucky Derby it would have been called a fast track.

Finally she stopped to wait for him. As he approached gasping for air, she said, "I think the road's this way."

He reached for her, grabbing only air as she was off again. He followed, trying to keep up. Her waving red hair was a torch in his blurry vision. He was too out of breath to even try to shout loudly enough for her to hear. Finally she stopped again. He slowed to a staggering walk and finally fell at her feet.

"Nobody's chasing us," He gasped. "Tell me again why we're running?"

She sat down. "I *saw* them. They're *horrible*. We need to get out of here. I was sure the road was over here somewhere. Maybe it's that way."

She started to get up and he grabbed her wrist. "Wait a minute. Wait a minute." Mark wheezed, "They aren't really horrible. I know they don't *look* too great…"

"They look *horrific*. Come, let's walk while we talk."

Mark looked about and realized it didn't matter which way they walked, they were hopelessly lost. Until they found that road, they wouldn't find Shrugg or their car. It did seem, however, that if they went on long enough they'd find either Shrugg, the road, or the highway. The highway would be the worst one to find, because they wouldn't know which way to follow it and it had been so bereft of traffic.

He'd caught his breath but his legs were weak. They walked hand-in-hand in the direction she choose.

"I had no idea you were such a runner," Mark laughed weakly. "I used to run track. Jeez, am I out of shape."

"I didn't know I was such a runner either. I just jog a few miles three times a week. I guess that's what a shot of adrenaline does."

"I have to start jogging with you. How'd you get here? I thought you were still in the car. Did you read my note?"

"No. I didn't see any note. I just woke up needing a bathroom and I guess I found the same one you used. Then there was this sign saying Shrugg was one mile, and a brand new blacktop road with your footprints on it. You'd only been gone a short while, so I figured I might catch up to you. I reached Shrugg and began walking around the edge of the town hiding behind tree trunks along the forest edge and I saw a couple of those creatures walking about and they scared the bejesus out of me. What are they?"

"While you slept in the car only an hour or two in Earth time, I've been in Shrugg a couple of days. Time moves differently here," Mark explained, and began recounting his visit to Shrugg as they walked. While he talked, worry gathered like dust in the far corners of his mind. If they were wandering in a different dimension, was there even a sliver of a chance they'd find a way out? He thought not, but it would do no good to worry her.

When they found a stream, they decided to follow it, hoping it was the same stream they both remembered flowing under the road. For some intuitive reason, they chose downstream to be the more likely way toward the road. When they'd followed it quite a while, they reached the top of a small waterfall. The stream ran to the edge of a cliff and fell ten feet to a beautiful blue pool below. They walked along the cliff's edge a short distance and found a place where they could climb down.

There beside the pool they found what Mark thought he'd seen from above, their dinner--two large bowls of fruit and vegetables and two large glasses of bubbly pink wine. He laughed out loud and felt himself relax inside.

"Gosh," she gushed. "Who'd leave this food here?"

"It was them," Mark explained. "Magoo said that if I ever went wandering around in the woods they'd follow 'til I wanted to go back to Shrugg."

"Gosh," she repeated and began eating.

They both ate their fill without emptying their bowls, and the wonderful wine made them giggly. Soon beth shed her clothes and ran into the pool with him close behind. In the waterfall's spray through a golden haze of evening they made love in a rainbow knee deep in cool water. The trout splashed around them then a light breeze licked them dry. Exhausted, they finally fell together on the bank, and drifted off, to sleep the warm night through in each other's arms.

The smell of eggs woke them early. Two full plates of steaming scrambles rested a few feet away with bowls of fruit and large glasses of orange juice.

"How the heck do you get *this* food to *this* place?" beth asked holding up her first forkful of eggs.

"Good question," Mark answered between bites. "Did I say the food's great?"

"Yes you did. And you didn't exaggerate, love."

After breakfast Mark finished of his visit to Shrugg.

"So you trust this Magoo, Mark?"

"Yes."

"Well, no use wasting any more of everybody's time with silly games." she laughed, reached over, took Magoo's beeper in her left hand, and pressed the button with her right thumb. [capital letter ↓]

"I'm curious to meet your Mister Magoo."

"Shall we get dressed, dear?" Mark asked.

"A final dip would sure be nice--a morning shower under the waterfall. It's not like they haven't seen us."

Magoo stepped into the clearing two minutes later with big white terrycloth towels over his arms. He threw Mark a large bar of soap saying. "Go ahead and use it. It's ecological."

Beth's first sight of Magoo put a big smile on her face that held back laughter.

Magoo smiled back, "I'll be downstream a bit, perhaps catching a few fish. You two take your time and beep me again when you're ready."

They used the soap and towels, then dressed and hit the beeper again in a few minutes.

"You didn't need to hurry," Magoo admonished when he appeared a minute later.

"Oh no, we're ready." Mark answered. "And we must say that you're the most amazing host ever, Magoo. I don't know how the heck you do it, but thank you very much. As hotels go you get five stars plus."

"Well, thank you, Mark. We do try. And we're practicing for future guests, also," Magoo replied, trying not to be obvious in his close study of beth, who in turn, couldn't take her eyes off this large funny shaped teddy bear with impeccable speech and the face of Mr. Magoo.

"And I want to explain how we got into this mess," Mark said. "Beth woke up, found the road and walked to

Shrugg. She saw some of your people and their appearance freaked her out. So, when she saw me out for a walk, she called out and began running through the woods. By the time I caught up to her to tell her we didn't need to run away, we were totally lost."

"I understand, Mark."

"I just wanted you to know I'm not quite ready to leave Shrugg yet, Magoo."

"I understand, Mark. Let's pick up this stuff and head back. It's a pretty long wa…"

Beth yelled out. She'd gone to retrieve her towel by the pool, tripped and fallen. They hurried over to help her up, but her ankle was hurt.

"Darn! The rock was slippery and it moved."

Magoo was fairly sure it was a sprain and not a break. That was good news, but she couldn't walk on it. He said he'd call for transportation.

"Don't fear of my assistant, beth. She won't harm you," Magoo said as a creature stepped from the trees.

Beth flinched slightly at the sight of the raccoon face with its big orange eyes, but managed to maintain a smile. Magoo wrote something on his pad, showed it to his assistant and then she made a call on something similar to a cell phone.

"Okay, transportation for you will be here in twenty-five minutes, beth. I can use a little rest. Shall we sit and talk while we wait?" Magoo suggested, settling his large frame down on a big rock beside the pool.

"So, Magoo," Mark started. "Do you *really* think my part of yesterday's meeting went well?"

"Oh, in some ways it didn't, but mostly it did. The poets got a huge laugh out of the fact that some of your people choose not to believe in science, and the scientists got back at them by laughing loudly when you said there were no poets on the councils. All of our meetings are loud like that, if that's what you're wondering."

"I'm wondering how seriously your council is considering exterminating earthlings to save the Earth."

"Welllll, I'm not saying that couldn't happen, but I'm against it and I think we'll make contact with earthlings soon to help you stop ruining the planet. Mostly what earthlings need to do quickly is harness solar power, quit destroying the rain forests and begin to make biodegradable plastics that don't ruin the oceans."

"Yeah. Those are things we've been working on."

"Yes, but meager efforts at a pitifully poor pace."

"I can't disagree with you there. Tell me, could they actually kill us off by peaceful means, as your council member put it? An oxymoron, if I ever heard one."

"Yes, we're pretty sure we can do that, Mark. Of course we've never done it before, but I think we could. Hopefully nobody will ever know for sure. It would be the easy way out. I think it would be a mistake though, and so far nearly all of the council members agree on that. We've made more than enough mistakes already with the clones."

"Oh yes, you said last night's meeting would go late after I left, and I assume the clone problems were the reason. Was anything decided?"

"No. There was endless discussion and no decisions. Excuse me, it's time I checked on the transportation."

Magoo stepped into the trees in the direction his assistant had gone. Mark wondered why he didn't just have his assistant come into the clearing to make the call. Perhaps he was having the creature stay out of sight a while in deference to beth, who wasn't yet comfortable with her appearance.

"Gee, Mark. He's amazing. That face, that voice. No wonder you named him Morgan Magoo. How do you suppose he got so fluent in English?"

"He told me he watched lots of movies, then managed to get hold of a dictionary, thesaurus and some English books. He's so smart. I bet he had them memorized in a few hours. In order to speak English he needed an operation to change his vocal chords though, and it left him unable to speak their language."

"Wow. Talk about dedicated. It must be pretty tough not being able to talk to anybody around him."

"Well he does still understand them. I think he's been teaching some of them to understand English, even though they can't speak it. How's your ankle doing?"

"Not so great. It's pretty painful. Look at it."

Mark agreed. It looked black and blue and swollen.

"I can't figure out what happened to that stone. I know I've stepped on it at least a couple times. Then this time it was like somebody moved it just as my weight..."

"Well, help is just a couple minutes away," Magoo announced stepping out of the trees with his assistant close behind. "Let me take another look at that ankle."

After another examination, Magoo was no longer so sure the ankle wasn't broken.

"What kind of transportation is it?" Mark asked.

"A rather primitive kind unfortunately. It'll be two girls with a stretcher and lots of ice."

Almost as if that was their stage prompt, the two burst out of the trees and stopped. One carried a stretcher, the other a large bag of ice and a small medical bag. Both were breathing very loudly.

"Okay. Let's give them a few minutes to catch their breath," Magoo said. "Then my assistant will go back with them--the three taking turns carrying the stretcher. I walk too slowly. The three girls can get beth to the clinic much faster than I can walk. Mark, you and I will bring up the rear, carrying all the dishes and towels and stuff. We'll get back to Shrugg an hour or two later."

Though Mark would rather have traveled with beth, Magoo's plan was the logical course of action. So a few minutes later the girls left, beth lying back on the stretcher, a towel full of ice around her ankle. Mark and Magoo soon followed, each carrying a few items. Magoo pointed the direction. There was no path. The forest appeared the same in all directions. Mark wondered how Magoo could be so sure of the way.

They hadn't walked more than two hundred yards in silence, Magoo slowing the pace considerably, when they had to stop and rest. Magoo was tired.

"I'm sorry to slow you down so, Mark. I'm really no spring chicken. I don't usually do so much walking. I traveled this way faster this morning."

Mark had seen no pathway they were following. He hoped the tired Magoo spoke metaphorically and was not hallucinating some path they were following off to some distant nowhere.

Magoo opened his medical bag, pulled out a green bandage and held it out to Mark saying, "Here, hold this a second please, and peel the wrapper off."

While Mark was peeling off the wrapper, Magoo bent down and Mark felt him pinch the back of his calf. He looked down and the spot on his leg was beginning to bleed.  {~ 9 ~}

## ~ 10 ~

## BAND AIDS ARE GREEN

"Now, you put that bandage on there, and I'll tell you what I just did and why I did it," Magoo said, opening a small bottle of clear liquid from his doctor bag. He placed a small piece of Mark's skin in it, tightened the lid back on and placed the bottle back in his bag.

"If we clone you, we'll use that piece of tissue to do it, Mark. I wanted to surprise you because the clone will inherit your memory bank and the less conversation about cloning and clone problems he remembers, the better. You won't be needing that beeper any more. Let me help you take it off."

"So he won't know he's a clone. He'll think he's me." Mark said, slipping the beeper over his head.

"If we decide we want him to, yes. Likely we'll grow him in the lab, then bringing him here to waken here with me." Magoo explained.

"How long does that take?"

"Only about ten hours of Shrugg time."

"But you're unsure whether you'll actually do it?"

"Yes. Some council members oppose making more clones for any reason, but I'm pretty sure we will."

"Who decides?"

"First the scientists decide what they want to do, then it goes before the council. No more clones are grown without a council vote."

"So I get no voice in the decision?"

"If you like, you can go before the council to make your wishes known. Do you *not* want to be cloned, Mark?"

"I don't know. Tell me about the problems you've been having with clones."

"Okay. I'll explain while we walk." Magoo said, standing up and pointing the way.

"You see, Mark, cloning was new science when we left our home planet. For the trip we made two clones for every self. Each self had an A-clone that hibernated nearly the entire journey. They wakened only a few times for maintenance, so they aged only a few weeks on the trip.

"Each self also had a B-clone on the trip. Two B-clones were awake on the ship at all times to do maintenance and assist the self in charge. So the B-clones were awake two days out of every 350. That meant they aged about forty years during the trip.

"The selfs hibernated too, so as to age minimally. Yet one of us had to be on duty running the ship all the time. There were 350 of us, so we were awake one day out of every three hundred and fifty. We selfs aged about twenty years. Actually by Earth time that would only be about seventeen years. Council members spent time having occasional meetings, so we aged an extra two months.

"So you see, when we arrived here, that meant each self had an A-clone twenty years younger than them and a B-clone twenty years older.

"It was all set up so we could monitor the health of our B-clone to predict our own future health problems. If your B-clone had a heart attack at age fifty, then you had to take preventative action before you reached fifty."

"You mean you'd harvest the heart of your A-clone."

"Perhaps, but only as a last resort. Harvesting organs from clones is the least desirable means to resolve health problems. It's not really ethical. During most of our trip we did it when necessary. Then we developed stem cell research. Now it's illegal to harvest organs from clones except in dire circumstances. Instead, we now get stem cells from our A-clones and use them to make new organs for selfs and for B-clones.

"So A-clones are really no longer essential--we could use our own stem cells. A-clones may help us solve our population problem, though. Clones aren't fertile, yet it's possible for a female clone to carry an implanted embryo to term. We got it to work once, but haven't been able to repeat that success.

"The main problems is that the clones want to vote. Also they're sterile yet have strong parenting instincts. Then there's the question of what to do with those who've had breakdowns, as well as how to deal with the B-clones' deep resentment at having wasted many years on the voyage.

"We can't let clones vote because they outnumber us two to one. The other problems we're working on."

"Can't you use stem cells to repair those with breakdowns?"

"If they were physical breakdowns we likely could. But they're mental problems. They grow paranoid and rebellious."

"Oh."

"Enough about problems, Mark. We can't solve them today. It's nearing time for you to end your little vacation in Shrugg. You said you weren't ready to leave when beth showed up. What do you still want to do here?"

"I need to know what I can do to help you make contact with earthlings, so we can work together to solve the Earth's problems."

"Well, your clone is what we needed to help us move in that direction. You've also given us invaluable information. We may contact you for more help, but you can rest easy tonight knowing you've already helped immensely."

"Uh yeah, about resting easy, Magoo. You know that bed in my house is about the most comfortable one I've ever slept in, but what's the trick to getting out of it?"

"You're having trouble with the bed?"

"Yeah. I sink down into it and it's so amazingly comfortable, but I can't seem to find any easy way to get out of it," Mark chuckled.

"We'll need to rethink the design." Magoo laughed. "It was designed just for you. You see our mattresses are much thinner. I see the problem. We thought a much thicker one would be good for you. We should have made it of a firmer material. It's too late now for you, but we'll adjust it for future guests."

"Why didn't you give me one like yours?"

"That wouldn't have worked at all. Lift me up, Mark."

"What?"

"Stand behind me and put your arms around my waist. Don't squeeze very tight, just lift me up."

Mark did as directed and began laughing. Magoo weighed all of ten, maybe twelve pounds.

"Jeez, Magoo, is everyone in Shrugg so light?"

"No. The women weigh almost three times as much. We all weigh a little more when we're younger. Now you know why I was fearful of you when we met. Had you put up any resistance I doubt that even the woman with me would have been much help."

"Yeah, I see."

"I did a pretty good Peter Lorre though, didn't I? I should have been an actor--that is if they had movies on our planet.

"You were a total ham, Magoo. A total ham. I should have wet my pants from laughing." Mark chided.

"Okay, okay, so I'm no Laurence Olivier." Magoo laughed. "Anyway, a mattress like mine wouldn't do for you or any future earthling guests. You know we're getting near Shrugg and I want to tell you about beth. She's a beautiful and wonderful girl but,...

Magoo's phone chose that moment to buzz loudly. He smiled, excused himself and answered it. Mark saw alarm in his face and then heard it in his voice when he said okay, he'd be right there.

"There's clone trouble." He explained hurriedly. "Let's go this way."

He pointed to the right and Mark followed him. Suddenly Magoo could move faster.

In a few seconds, ahead Mark saw the end of the blacktop road he'd walked to get to Shrugg. Through the trees, on the right, he could see Shrugg and black smoke was billowing from one of the buildings. Creatures were running about, making loud, high pitched gibberish. He and Magoo stopped by the end of the road. Magoo bent over and, struggling for breath, pointed down the road.

"Run!" he gasped.

"But beth!" Mark shouted.

"She's safe! You need to trust me on that! I must hurry!"

"Come with me!"

"I belong here!" Magoo called over his shoulder, turning to hobble toward Shrugg.

Mark turned and began running on the road away from Shrugg. He had to pace himself. He'd been a quarter miler in track, not a long distance man. Beth had shown him how far out of shape he was. He slowed to a jog. As much as he wanted to get away fast and bring back help, it was paramount that he actually get away. How did Magoo know beth was safe? And safe for how long? She was in the clinic. How did Magoo know that was a safe place? How could he be so sure?

When he reached the stream, Mark scrambled down to it and drank deeply. He hurried back up to the road and pushed his rubbery legs onward. His pace slowed even more. How had he let himself get so out of shape? Finally he was walking. He walked as fast as he could. What would he do at the car? First leave a marker beside the road so he could find Shrugg again. It had to be visible. Spare tire? No, he'd need that if he had a flat. The "Shrugg, 1 Mile" sign. Yeah, along with the cooler. He'd set his odometer too. Magoo said his car would start, so Mark was sure it would. But Magoo said Beth would be there in the car asleep and that sure wasn't going to happen. So Magoo's sight into the future wasn't quite 20/20. He'd try his phone and keep on trying it as he drove, 'til he got through. To who? Ahhhhh Tom. He'd try Tom. Get him to bring some guys--cousins, brothers, workers from the restaurant. Have 'em bring baseball bats, ~~mostly~~ for self defense. No one at Shrugg was strong and he didn't think there were any weapons. Just a few guys would do it. Maybe he'd have been strong enough by himself. How many of them were there?

Mark spied the end of the road and the back of the sign. He resumed running. The sign didn't come out easily. He worried it back and forth, then pulled and it came. He tucked it under his arm, ran across the deep grass to the car and saw Beth asleep on the front seat. Mark stared through the open window at her. His hand trembled on the door handle. He was leaning down catching his breath as tears welled up in his eyes. How had Magoo done it? He must have sent her here instead of to the clinic? Why? He'd seemed so surprised about the clone rebellion. How had he known? Why had he kept her whereabouts a secret from Mark? Magoo had been saying something about Beth when his phone rang. He must have been about to tell Mark that she was here in the car.

Mark dropped the sign. It landed facing up. He read, *Privit Propity, Keep Owt*. He shook his head and smiled, then noticed that the highway sign by the car now said "Hwy 72 East". His rubbery legs wobbled him around to the driver's door. He was worried about Beth's ankle. It hadn't received medical attention. He couldn't see it up under the dashboard. She slept peacefully though.

Beth awoke as Mark got behind the wheel, though he closed his door as quietly as possible. She sat up rubbing the sleep from her eyes and asked, "Are we there yet?"

Mark looked at her, puzzled. "No. How's your ankle doing?"

"My ankle? Why? Is there something wrong with my ankle?"

"It was hurt. Let me see."

Beth lifted both her legs and put her feet on Mark's lap. Amazingly neither ankle was the least bit swollen or discolored. Then, as she lifted her legs to put them back down, Mark glimpsed a green Band Aid and relief flooded through him.

"Say, where'd you get that green Band Aid?"

Beth looked down and saw it on the back of her calf. "I don't know. Did you put it there? Are you playing games, Mark?"

He smiled. "Nope. Leave it on. I'll tell you all about it tomorrow morning. I'm just too tired to start in on it now."

He wished he could take her to that waterfall by the cool, sleepy pool. It was hard to believe she hadn't been there with him yesterday.

"I'm afraid it's getting too late to swim." he said as he pulled out onto the highway, "I saw a school a while back as we were driving. You know, I bet they have an empty playground in back with some nice swings we could swing on and watch the sunset."

"Sounds romantic, Mark, but I don't know if I should. Mama told me all about boys like you. You just wanna peek up under a girl's dress. I know your tricks." She smiled, while under her skirt her thumbs slipped beneath the elastic waistband of her panties.

"Who me?" He grinned and shrugged.

~THE END~

## ~ WRITER'S BLOG ~

    I was inspired to write *Shrugg, 1 Mile* while reading *Keegan's End,* an Ebook by Chris Kwapich. I thank Chris, a talented young story teller with much potential and a plethora of fresh ideas.
    I started this book April 29th, 2014 and finished the first draft on June 15$^{th}$. I'd penned songs, poetry, short stories, journalism, a nonfiction book and a children's book. This was my first completed full length book of fiction and my first attempt at science fiction. As fast and easy as it seems to have been in retrospect, facing all those blank pages ahead was as daunting as viewing those full pages behind was exciting. I don't foresee a large amount of editing ahead, but there's always a certain amount.
    The book was about 25% along, I was struggling with exactly what to say next and how to say it, when it occurred to me that it would be fun to write the ending. So I then wrote the final few paragraphs of the book-- paragraphs wherein I changed only two words when I

reached that ending. Having that final plot twist on paper didn't make the writing easy, but made it more doable.

This book was also made possible by my wife, Susanna's, encouragement. She's a voracious reader and generally my toughest critic. After I convinced her to peruse the first few chapters, she went on to read the pages one-by-one as they fell from the printer. It was as though we were reading and enjoying the book together, both quite excited by it.

There's the question of a sequel. The smashwords Epublished version of this book has garnered encouraging reviews, (see some on the back cover of this book) so I've begun a sequel. I doubt it will be completed soon, however. I have ideas for the beginning and middle, but none yet for a final ending twist. I loved the ending I found for this book, but I can't use the same one twice. That would be cheating--not to mention boring.

I feel that I've set a fairly high bar with *Shrugg, 1 Mile*. The sequel must measure up very near it, and that may take a while. I've penned the first chapter and part of the second chapter of that sequel though, and I thought I'd share a portion of them here, because I thought you'd enjoy them, and on the off chance that I never reach that elusive finish line: *(It's the morning after. Over breakfast, Mark has been telling Beth about his visit to Shrugg)"*

"And you *really* thought that girl you made love to in Shrugg was me?"

"Of *course* I did. You know clones are exact replicas, right? She even had all your memories and thoughts. *I* thought she was you, and I'm sure *she* thought she was you. I had no idea a clone of you even existed until I found you back at the car and saw the green band aid they left on your calf."

"But they aren't quite *exact* replicas, are they?"

"They can't have children, they can't be cloned, in Shrugg they can't vote and their names aren't capitalized. Other than that, they're quite exactly like the self they duplicate." Mark explained.

"So what about the time thing, Mark? If we see them a year from now, how old will they be?"

"I hadn't thought about that either,...I suppoooose..... they'll be roughly sixteen years older than us."

Beth sipped her latte. They ate scrambled eggs and toast while their minds scrambled in countless directions.

"So there's nothing we should do, is there?" Beth finally half-whispered.

"Nothing we *could* do, as far as I can see. Who'd believe us if we tried to tell them about it? Magoo was right when he said you aren't a witness. You only believe me because you know me. And we have no idea how to get back to Shrugg or contact Magoo."

"What if we tried to find our way back?"

"Even if we could find that spot on that highway, I don't think the road to Shrugg would be there. It seems to appear and disappear whenever Magoo wishes. I'm not even sure when we entered their dimension. It may have been when we turned onto that weird North Highway."

"But how did I fall asleep on that highway and wake up back on US 72?"

"I have no idea how Magoo managed that."

"And how the *heck* did we just happen to show up there by the road into Shrugg, Mark? It's not like we *wanted* to go there or were *looking* for it or anything."

"We'd have to ask Magoo about that one too. It all seems to have been planned by him. I'm sure this had a lot to do with it though." Mark suggested, pulling the small pen from his shirt pocket. He rolled it in his fingertips like a small cigar, studying its "Shrugg Inn" inscription, and feeling that slight tingle.

"Do you really trust this Magoo, Mark?"

"Yeah,...yeah I'm pretty sure I do."

"But he cloned us without our permission. And now our clones are his prisoners. Why did he make them, and what's will he do with them? They're in a strange world, with no way to escape and really nowhere to escape to."

"Yeah, but there's a bigger picture too, Beth. People in Shrugg see us trashing this world where they came to make a new home. Some of them want to go the easy way, erase us, and have this world to themselves. Apparently they can do it. Magoo favors their only alternative--stopping us from polluting the world to death, and peacefully coexisting with us. Our clones are part of his plan to help him move in that direction."

"But you said the clones in Shrugg are rebelling. Could making two more be a step in the right direction?"

` "Well, Magoo seems awfully smart. He apparently planned out my trip to Shrugg and now has the clones he wanted. It leaves us with lots of questions, but they're questions bound to go unanswered until we hear from Magoo. If we do ever hear from him. But we need to try to set this whole thing aside for now. It's even possible that the clone rebellion that was starting when I left, put an end to Shrugg, so my clone never got created. And your clone could have died along with Magoo and everyone else in Shrugg. In that case, we'll never hear anything. So let's at least *try* to get our minds back to this dimension. It's Monday morning, and you have class in an hour."

"I don't know how I'll concentrate in class, but you're right, we have to get on with our lives. Do you have plans for today?"

"Yeah. I refuse to waste my day off work sitting around thinking and worrying about Shrugg. I thought I might give you a ride to school, then check out a realtor or two. When I pick you up after class, maybe we could go look at some apartments together,"

"Apartments? hmmmmm," She teased, pretending not to have the slightest notion of his intentions.

"Yep, apartments. Neither of us has a place big enough for us both, so I figure we should go see what's available. Ya think?"

"Gee, I think it's going to be absolutely *impossible* to concentrate in class today."

The friendly rental agent lady, pointing out the bathroom's generous size and modern fixtures, wasn't privy to a discrete pat of Beth's left cheek, an answering squeeze of his right cheek, or their glanced meeting of eyes. She caught the slight upward curl of their lips though, and took it as approval of the amenities, which it was,...at least partly.

That night at 1:02 AM, Beth's stressed out, too small bed gave up and collapsed beneath them--the last straw. They took the apartment. Her sleep deprived neighbors, Joe and Phil, while professing disappointment, harbored a droll appreciation of their departure.

\* \* \*

Viewed from above, thunderclouds resemble ponderous anvils. From below they're fierce, greenish darkness blotting out the light from all heavenly orbs. Mark's first encounter with Magoo had been a thundercloud, severely dark, but steady in its passing. His visit to Shrugg was a thin, nagging mist about his feet--a slightly uncomfortable chill creeping in to stay an indefinite while.

Though witness to neither event, Beth owned not an iota of doubt. As she had shared the darkness, so too, she knew the mist and felt a disquieting chill.

CHAPTER 2

As they walked, mark grew more doubtful that Magoo knew the way back to Shrugg. He couldn't discern the slightest trace of path, just a hazy maze of tall trees as far as the eye could see. But Magoo was in good spirits as he hiked slowly along, stopping often to rest. He passed the time telling mark about his years spent traveling to Earth, and how strange it had been to spend each day working, then sleep a year-long night that in most ways felt no longer than any normal night. He described some funny things that had happened along the way, and mentioned that a few scary and sad things had too, but went into no details there. Magoo's navigation was fine though, and near dusk the Shrugg clearing hove into view.

*(To be continued.)*
\* \* \*\* \* \* \* \* \* \* \* \* \* \* \* \* \* \* \* \* \* \* \* \* \* \* \* \* \*

Reviews *are* appreciated. Please post a review on Amazon or on goodreads. A few words, or six paragraphs--whatever. (Think of it as a gift.) You needn't consider yourself an expert. There are no experts.

I apologize for typos or punctuation errors I may have missed. Please inform me of any you see (but please not the failure to capitalize clone names) at *gregsdaylily@hotmail.com*. A great thing about modern publishing is the ease of making corrections to effect future copies.

**Other books by G. A. Schindler:**

"**Footprints**"--a book of poetry, songs and humor, is available as a createspace paperback on Amazon and may soon be available on Kindle.

"**Love is the Smile**"--a creative nonfiction book for young adults about sex in long term relationships, is an Ebook on smashwords, and a createspace paperback on Amazon.

"**Great Speckled Banana's Great Quest**"--a humorous book "for children from 3 to 103," is a createspace paperback available on amazon.

"**Timmy and the Hotdog Song**"--also a humorous children's book, is another createspace paperback available on amazon.

"**A Blaze A Glory**"--a createspace paperback book of short stories is also available on amazon

Made in the USA
Charleston, SC
04 April 2015